The adventures of
Bruce from Bondi

Written and illustrated by Steve McGregor

STEVE MCGREGOR BOOKS

This is a work of fiction. Names, characters, places, and incidents either are the product of the author's imagination or are used fictitiously. Any resemblance to actual persons, living or dead, events, or locales is entirely coincidental.

ISBN 978-0-6453543-3-1

SECOND EDITION

Dedication

Dedicated to all of my mates who remember the Australian hotels during the 1950's and who may have enjoyed their breakfasts.

Contents

Foreword

The first book titled "Adventures of a Jackeroo" is about our hero and is the story of Bruce a hapless gormless youth. Due to his loathing of anything to do with school he had a rush of blood to the head and fled to Enngonia way out west in the state of New South Wales where he was taken on as a Jackeroo. For those who don't know a Jackeroo is a trainee drover and sheep station manager here in Australia.

However, Bruce as a Jackeroo shows that not all of us are born with brains or able to be smooth and accomplish great things. Bruce is a fish out of water, a city boy struggling to be a man in the Australian countryside of the 1950's when it was still pretty rough. Fortunately for Bruce he does eventually come good and we will see how he accomplished this.

In the last chapter of the book Bruce gets lucky. He returns to his beloved Bondi and meets a beautiful girl whose father owns a pub and was offered a job in her father's hotel. Well Bruce immediately thinks that this would be a great step forward much better than sitting in the saddle under the blazing sun playing foster father to a mob of silly sheep and accepts the position.

He of course imagined that being a trainee hotel manager would be plain sailing compared to the hard life on a sheep station but when you read this book you will soon see that he was wrong. Hotels are host to many different types of people and the characters that Bruce meets along the way sometimes give him cause for complaint. In fact we can well imagine that Bruce on occasions would think it may have been better to have stayed way out west on Booleroo Sheep station where it was a whole lot more peaceful.

The noise of the Salvation Army band, the lady stuck in the bathtub, Greta the Alsatian dog eating all the hotel's sausages and the inebriated professor standing on the bar spouting verse are just some of the amusing tales told. Have a read of "The Adventures of Bruce from Bondi" and see how he copes with some of these situations.

These two books are published on Amazon and other eBook readers. Just look up "Adventures of a

Jackeroo" or the author "Steve McGregor" and you will find your way.

Go to www.amazon.com/dp/B00K1I5Y8O to find more books about Bruce From Bondi.

Cast of Characters

Banjo Patterson – an Australian poet

Barry the Bard – a professor of literature from the University.

Bruce – the hero of our story, sometimes called Brucie

Bill – Bill the Barman, the barman, sometimes called Billie

Blackie - one of Bruce's mates, named Blackie due to his dark complexion.

Bondi Beach – not a person but it makes its presence felt

Bluey – ex drover and now fish shop specialist.

Chalky – one of the regulars at the hotel

Cookie – the cook who regularly knocks off the cooking sherry

Dorothy Mackellar – Australian poet

Flipper – the one armed hotel cleaner. Because he had only one arm

Frankie – one of the regulars at the hotel who has a run in with a stray dog

Greta – The Alsatian dog (German Shephard), she loves Bruce

Gazzer – the paper boy

Hori – one of the Maori drinkers

Henry Lawson — an Australian poet

Jackie — the aboriginal tracker from Engonnia.

Jacko — The cook at Booleroo Sheep Station, a real monster

Jane — the publican's daughter and Bruce's true love

Lloyd Price — American singer of Bruce's favourite song – 'Personality'.

Macca — one of the regulars at the hotel

Maurie the Maori — a huge Maori from New Zealand

Milly — the housemaid, who tidies and cleans the rooms

Mr. Walter Brownstone MP — the local politician, a member of parliament

Mr. Cavalier — The Manager of the hotel, with the nick name of 'Smiley'

Mr. Reginald Campbell-Smythe — an English guest (The Pommie) at the hotel who didn't like his breakfast

Mrs. Greatley — a guest of the hotel who was stuck in the bath

Mr. Poleford - the guest in room 8 who "died"

Mrs. Potter — a lady in the Saloon Bar who teases Bruce

Porky — one of the regulars at the hotel

Salvoes – Sallies — The Salvation Army, much loved and respected in Australia

Sammy — The SP Bookie takes off course bets from the regulars

O'Flaherty — the owner of the mad cow in Enngonia, Bruce had a ride on her

Skeeter – one of Bruce's mates from Booleroo sheep station

Smiley – the Manager of the Auckland Hotel, Bondi, see Mr. Cavalier

Stinker – one of the regulars at the hotel who dives into an empty swimming pool

The Captain- The leader of the Salvation Army band

The Boys from Booleroo – Whippy, Blackie, Skeeter, Jackie (the aboriginal tracker),

Whippy - one of Bruce's mates,

Willy - (Wully) the bagpiper from Scotland

Wee Wully – Little Willy, the little boy with the long kilt.

Cast of Characters Album

This album shows a few of the many characters that inhabit the world of Bruce from Bondi. When you dive into the book you will meet them all and after seeing their faces here you will be well acquainted with them when they crop up in the story.

Bruce – The Trainee Hotel Manager

Jane - Bruce's sweetheart

Maurie - a giant Maori from New Zealand

Milly – the Hotel's Maid

Greta the Alsatian – who loves sausages

Wee Wullie – from Scotland

Whippy – a mate from the country

Mrs. Greatley — who was stuck in the bath

The Captain — Bondi Salvation Army band

The Hotel's Cook — into the cooking sherry

Barry the Bard – the Professor in full flight

Mrs. Potter – from the Ladies Saloon Bar

Jackie - the Aboriginal Tracker

Bluey – ex drover and now Fish Shop manager

The Boys from Booleroo – some of Bruce's mates

Bill the Barman and **Smiley** the Manager

Mr. Poleford – the guest in room 8

The Sallies – the Bondi Band

Chapter 1

Bruce from Bondi

Although Bruce was raised in Bondi, a suburb of Sydney near the famous Bondi Beach, he was until recently working in the country. A few years earlier he would have done anything to escape the confines of school where he thought there was nothing left to teach him as he thought he knew it all. As luck would have it Bruce got a job as a Jackeroo near Enngonia in the State's far west. Out there on Booleroo Sheep Station life was tough learning how to manage a property running sheep and it was hot, very dry and the flies during the day made his life a misery. He managed to endure the three years there and on his first holiday from the sheep and the flies he returned home to Mum and Dad for a week. Little did he know that the week's end would not see him return to Booleroo.

What happened was that he decided to stroll on down to Bondi Beach and as he loved it so much he joined the famous Bondi life-saving club. When he was filling out the application form the girl in the office caught his eye. In fact Jane was beautiful and really the girl of his dreams. Imagine his pleasure when he also found that Jane's father owned a hotel at Bondi and it was only a little while later that he found himself going to start working there and learning the ropes how to be a trainee hotel manager.

Bruce found that for some unaccountable reason Jane liked him and Jane's shadow a very large

1

Alsatian dog called Greta adored Bruce. It did not take Bruce long to work out that while he liked dogs he loved girls more, well at least in a different way. In fact he very much loved Jane and he couldn't be happier. It certainly was a whole lot better living in Sydney by the sea and starting work in relative comfort. What put the icing on the cake, so as to speak, was that Jane's Dad owned The Auckland Hotel and Bruce basked in the glow of a young woman's affection while enjoying all the benefits of working in an Australian Pub.

Jane was a corker of a girl. Not too tall and certainly not too short. Blond haired and blue eyed with a beautiful figure that filled her one piece bathing suit out in all the right places. In addition to the loveliness of the girl she was blessed with a sunny loving nature and a sense of humour where of all things she laughed at Bruce's weak attempts at humour and in fact thought him uproariously funny.

"I had better get on in and wake Bruce up, I don't want him to be late on his first day," said Bruce's Mum to the second in charge, Bruce's Dad, Big Phil.

"Yes dear," was the muffled reply as Big Phil buried his head further into the Sydney Morning Herald and gave the pages a shake as if to say "bloody women always telling me what to do."

It was Bruce's first day alright, at his new job as trainee manager of the Auckland Hotel, which was close by just down the road and around the corner. That morning his mother banged on his bedroom door and put her head around to make sure he was awake. Imagine her surprise when she saw him sitting on his bed already dressed and ready to start the day.

He had already purchased a white shirt, smart black lace up shoes and black socks for the job, from

Gowings men's store in the city, and found the new clobber a good deal different from his moleskin trousers, bush shirt, wide hat and elastic sided work boots that were his usual apparel in his previous job as Jackeroo.

Whacko Bruce is back from the bush at his beloved Bondi beach

"My goodness Bruce you are up early, it's not like you to be up and about at this hour," said his Mum in amazement but pleased to see that her darling son had matured and was taking some responsibility.

Bruce peered up at his mother and did not say what he was thinking and instead hiding his irritation said "Mum I think you've forgotten that for the last three years I have been working up the bush and all the drovers started early so I have just got used to it. Mind you I never slept a wink last night, I just lay there thinking about my new job and I couldn't close my eyes."

"Never mind Bruce, it won't be long now, anyhow Dad has something for you son as a present for you on your first day at the hotel. Come on down to the kitchen and you will see what we have for you."

Bruce slowly got to his feet and followed his mother's bustling figure down the hall to the kitchen where his father was sitting with his back to the wall. On entering the room Big Phil looked up and put the newspaper he was reading to one side.

"Hello son, your Mum and I have bought you a gift to celebrate your first day and here it is," and he bent down and pulled out a briefcase from under his chair.

"We thought that as you were going to be in management you could do with a briefcase to look the part."

All this was said while Bruce's parents beamed at him. Bruce was pleased with the gift and thought it was a bit different from the saddle bags he was used to up at Booleroo.

"Crikey Mum and Dad what a beaut present that will do the trick that's for sure. I can carry me lunch in it too."

Bruce sat down to have his Kellogg's Corn Flakes and toast and Vegemite and in no time was ready to get moving on the next chapter in his life.

"Bye Mum n Dad", said Bruce and with his loving parent's good wishes ringing in his ears was soon striding down the footpath heading for his new job and stopping off on the way for a short while to see his beloved Bondi beach.

Bruce was living very close by the famous surfing beach at Bondi and in a short time the booming sound of the surf came to his ears. He stopped at the wall overlooking the beach and stood there taking in the sights. He had plenty of time before he was expected to report for work on his first day at the hotel.

Bruce just stood there and took a deep breath and let it our slowly. It was early morning and the sun was well and truly above the horizon and all the seagulls were wheeling and dive bombing each other as they frolicked in the cool onshore breeze.

The smell of the ocean was strong on the air as Bruce and other early risers took advantage of the quiet time before the tourists and sunbathers moved in. He gazed idly at a young couple strolling along by the water's edge and dodging the rollers as they washed up on the shore in a lather of foam. Just a little further towards the south end of the beach the old guys who were called the Ice Bergs, were also up bright and early and the elderly overweight men were laughing and joking as they trudged along to the rock lined swimming pool for their early morning dip.

Bruce sighed and breathed in a great lungful of ozone saturated air and thought out loud, "Jeez this is for me, why did I ever leave you? Well I gotta get to work and it's my first day at the pub, so I'd better get goin' I don't want to be late."

He was all dolled up and ready to go to work

In no time he had arrived and with his heart thumping and feeling rather nervous Bruce entered the dim interior of the main bar. He saw no one and made his way down the hall to the back of the hotel and saw a light on in the office.

Jane was there sitting at a desk and when she saw him jumped up from where she was reading a magazine and gave him a big hug and kiss on the cheek. "There you are and don't you look all smart with a collar and tie."

"Jeez thanks Jane you look pretty good too and this collar is strangling me," as Bruce ran a finger around the inside of his collar and stuck his tongue out and rolled his eyes as if he was being choked.

Jane giggled and said, "Come and meet Smiley, Mr. Cavalier, who is the manager of the hotel. He will have something organised for you so you can learn the ropes."

"I can guess why they call him 'Smiley" it's coz he smiles a lot.

"Wrong, it's because he doesn't smile at all, that's why!" laughed Jane as she beckoned him to follow her as she walked down the stairs to the cellar beneath the hotel.

In the dim light Bruce made out wooden kegs lining the wall and tubes and taps going up into the roof and disappearing from view. A voice greeted them and out of the gloom the manager appeared with his hand outstretched in greeting. Bruce took the proffered hand and shook it while he greeted Smiley as Jane introduced them.

Bruce saw before him a stern faced man with a face dominated by a dark moustache not much older than himself. In no time he was made to feel comfortable and in fact everyone was so friendly Bruce soon forgot his nervousness and his heart rate had slowed down to normal thumping.

Bruce was shown where to put his gear and his new briefcase, with its sole contents of two peanut butter sandwiches and an apple, and was asked to follow Smiley further into the cellar where the pipes were.

Jane fluttered her fingers at Bruce and said, "See you later Bruce, we can have lunch as soon as you are given the word to have a break, just come upstairs and see me when you can."

"Sounds good Janie, see you and Greta real soon."

Smiley stood there with his arms folded looking at Bruce and asked him if he had any experience in working in a hotel and when he was informed that Bruce knew nothing he pushed out his lower lip and thought awhile.

"Well Bruce I reckon we can start you off from the bottom up so as to speak. I will show you how to bring the kegs of beer in when they are delivered. Hook 'em up to the lines and you will see later that the beer will flow up to the taps up at the bar ready for the lunch time rush. Later we can get you to work in the bar, then the kitchen and also carry a tray. How does that sound? First though I will take you around to meet all the crew."

All this was very new to Bruce and he stood there as all new chums do at a new job and thought to himself that he would never learn any of it let alone remember it and he would be dismissed for being an idiot.

With a sinking feeling that he would fail and have to go back and work out in the bush again,

So all Bruce could say in a strangled voice was, "Sounds good to me Mr. Cavalier I will give it a go."

Chapter 2

Bruce Learns the Ropes

Smiley the hotel manager beckoned Bruce over to where he was standing. There was a large beer keg, one of three standing in a row in the gloom of the cellar like three squat idols on an altar.

"Now Bruce I will show you one of the cellarman's jobs which is to hook up a keg to the lines supplying the beer to the taps upstairs, so follow what I do."

The bar manager quickly gave him a run through on what to do and how to handle everything. However, as usual when someone is showing you a new job they tend to rush it and Smiley gabbled away and Bruce just stood there and absorbed about half of what he was told.

"Now Bruce when they call down from upstairs just unhook the lines from the old keg. Then broach the new keg and then hook her up so they can get a flow of beer."

"But Smiley what if something goes wrong?"

"Nah it's simple mate, nothing will go wrong, I will leave you to it and just call out if you want anything," and with that Smiley disappeared into the semi darkness leaving an uncomfortable Bruce still with his two questioning hands raised in the air.

Standing there in the stale beer smelling cellar Bruce peered around him in the near dark and thought that Smiley reckoned the job was easy but he was still not too sure of what to do. He turned to walk over to the boxes of port, sherry and soft drink stacked on the floor when he heard a sound behind him and Jane's dog Greta ambled up to him wagging her tail for a pat. Bruce brightened up when he saw the friendly face of Greta and thought that she would be good company compared to some of the types upstairs in the main bar. As a conversation opener Greta smiled her doggie smile and rolled over on her back to have her stomach rubbed.

"Hang on Greta don't go away I think I am needed".

Someone from the main bar upstairs was thumping on the floor to get his attention to change kegs and Bruce abandoned his companion who by this time had decided to search for a flea that was bothering her. Bruce pushed past Greta to get a better look at where the lines were on the old keg which he quickly tugged free.

He grabbed the mallet and looked at the new keg. "OK all I've gotta do is to loosen the plug from the hole and hook up the new tube things so the beer flows upstairs through the whatchermacallits to the taps. Now that can't be hard can it Greta?"

Greta gave a few thumps of her tail on the floor and grinned at Bruce, all teeth and red tongue.

A voice echoed down from above, "Hey Brucie c'mon willya hook 'er up and let's get the beer flowing."

Bruce gave a half-hearted hit of the mallet to the keg and woggled and wiggled at the bung to open the keg for the beer. Suddenly the plug came free and with a whoosh and a roar a column of beer exploded out of the hole and hit Greta who was by this time happily decimating the flea population on her flanks.

The happy and contented dog was suddenly drenched with cold beer and was lost to sight for a few moments as the torrent of beer foamed. Poor old

Greta let out a yelp, put her tail between her legs and shot through as fast as her legs could carry her.

Bruce popped the cork and whoosh went the beer and Greta took off.

For a short time Bruce stood there with his mouth open while the force of the beer eventually slowed and with an effort of will he picked up the lines and forced them into the plug hole to halt the flow and pumped away to give the keg more pressure.

"Jeez what am I goin' to do now? The place stinks of beer and is awash with the stuff. I wonder how I can get outta this one?"

Bruce hunted around and eventually found a mop and a bucket and set to as fast as he could to soak up all the puddles of beer and foam before someone came down to the cellar and saw the mess the place was in.

"Crikey, I wonder how long the keg will last now that half of the flaming stuff is on the floor, when they ask for another keg I hope I get it all hooked up before it goes everywhere."

For a while all the sounds from the cellar were a swishing and a sloshing of beer. "I must find out what I did wrong there with that flamin' keg, I have got the sneaking suspicion that Smiley left out a few things that I had to do to get the beer flowing properly."

Later that afternoon Smiley ran down the stairs and saw Bruce stacking the shelves and generally tiding up. "That's looking good Bruce, well done, how about you have a go tomorrow at the main bar. We can show you how to pull the beers and ring up the change in the till, an all. Whaddya reckon?"

"Thanks Smiley, I seem to have got the knack of it down here in the cellar so I'm game for having a go at another job."

The next day Bruce arrived at the Auckland Hotel nice and early and donned a waistcoat and swapped his tie for a bow tie and was ready to do battle.

Bill the barman had the job of showing Bruce how to pull a beer and soon the drink orders were coming fast and the beer was flowing. Bruce was getting the hang of it and was able to ring up the change in the cash register and was getting along quite well.

Later that afternoon Bill asked Bruce to call down to the cellarman to change the kegs and he waited until the answering shout from below said that all was ready to go.

He grabbed the tap handle and pulled and it was then that the beer in the new lines rushed out and a stream of white froth went everywhere.

Bruce pulled the handle and the beer and froth went everywhere.

Bruce just stood there with his mouth open looking at the mess and shouted, "Stone the bloody crows willya look at that, Jeez, it's not my fault Billie mate."

Bill swung around to see the bar awash with foam and more was coming. The regulars breasting the bar had jumped back and one shouted, "Strike a light

Brucie willya let go of the tap and stop wasting good beer!"

Bill quickly took over and pushed the lever up to stop the flow of froth and there was then dead silence in the bar as everybody looked to see the clouds of foam that were subsiding until Bruce and Bill were only up to their knees in the stuff.

Above the shouts and yells of advice and encouragement from the wags in the bar Bruce managed to blurt out, "Crikey Bill what the hell happened?"

"Don't worry Bruce I reckon it is the idiot cellarman having a go, it's his sense of humour you see. Every time we have a new barman he stokes the kegs with as much gas as he can pump in and whoosh, you can see the result."

"What a joker, he almost gave me the fright of my life, I thought the stuff would never stop and we would be breathing froth and drown in the stuff."

"Yeh, it's a waste of good beer alright. I will just go downstairs and sort him out. Hang on up here and hold the fort while one cellarman gets an ear full."

Bruce was preparing to clean up some of the residue of the froth when a dark figure loomed. One of the aboriginals from the city had dropped into the bar and wanted to place an order.

"What will it be mate?" asked Bruce with a smile as he wiped a bit of froth off the cash register.

The man leaned over the bar and looked furtively around him. "Hey cobber can I have I have six bottles of Port?" came the whispered reply.

"Yeh, no problems a half dozen of Mr. Penfold's best Royal Reserve coming up. Do you want a hand carrying it?"

14

"Shh, keep it down, I can carry it brudder and I have a few of my mates outside and they will do the job," replied the dark man quietly as he looked around again swiftly and then proffered a twenty pound note and waited for his change.

As soon as the bottles were handed over and the man took his change he slipped quickly away and left Bruce standing there ready to serve another customer.

Bill had just returned from his visit to the cellarman and saw the aboriginal leaving with the bottles and shook his head at Bruce.

"You had better not sell any more of that stuff to the aboriginal lads Bruce, they are not supposed to drink any grog unless we know them."

"Right you are Bill I will speak with you first next time, there seems to be more to this job than I thought."

Chapter 3

Maurie the Maori

Bruce was rather enjoying working at the hotel in Bondi and could see why some called it God's country. To make matters even better he was in love and the object of his affection was Jane the Publican's daughter. Also for reasons that escaped him Jane loved Bruce and after all he reasoned that's all that mattered.

It was a far cry living in the mild climate of Bondi with its cool onshore breezes compared to where he had recently worked far out west in the desiccated countryside around Enngonia.

His companions were his fellow drovers and Jackeroos plus the ten thousand sheep and a million or more flies. The flies seemed to like buzzing around humans and the couple of black crows, who lived in the eucalyptus gum trees down by the tank, always appeared to be following him around.

He was leaning on the counter of the bar day-dreaming about the life he lived until recently when he heard ...

"Kia Ora Bro gimme a beer," in a soft voice.

Bruce looked up and saw before him a mountain of a man, lightly coloured who was at least close to seven feet. He was a big fellow around the middle too as a large roll of lard spread over his belt. Bruce thought for a fleeting second of the size of the mad cow owned by O'Flaherty out at Enngonia and shook his head to bring himself back to the present.

"Why sure mate", squeaked Bruce. "What wouldja like and where are you from?"

The giant smiled and said, "I'm from the 'Land of the Long White Cloud' bro and me and me mates are over here for a game of footie."

Bruce saw before him a monster, but he looked a friendly monster

"Ah, youse must be a Maori that right?"

"Yis call me Maurie and who are you?"

"Just call me Bruce mate and I'm from Booleroo out near Enngonia but now I live down here safe from all them wild kangaroos and things, smirked Bruce bunging on a bit of an act which was entirely lost on Maurie the Maori."

After all the Maori's, the native people of New Zealand, are a race of warriors and would have no fear at all of any mythical wild Kangaroo and would most probably either play Rugby with them or eat them, although they would have cooked them first of course.

The man mountain from New Zealand smiled a gap toothed grin and scratched his wavy hair. "What kind of beer hev you got, bro?"

Bruce gulped again looking at the huge 280 pound warrior from the south land of New Zealand and rattled off a list of beers that were available.

The giant shook his head and asked, "None of that Aussie stuff bro how about good Kiwi brew like Stein Lager, that will gev you a kuck?"

Bruce found three lonely bottles of Stein Lager beer in the freezer and opened a bottle for the giant who quickly guzzled down half of the cold brew and set the bottle down with a loud clunk on the bar.

"Thit was super," said Maurie the Maori with a wide gapped toothed grin and before Bruce could reply there was a loud stampede of crashing feet and the jostling of bodies, just like a herd of bulls back on Booleroo, when the doors to the bar opened and the rest of the Maori football team entered. All dwarfed Bruce and some were even bigger than Maurie.

Bruce managed to say over the jostling mass of Maori bodies and shouted orders for drinks, just to pass the time.

"What position do you play in footie mate?"

Maurie mentioned he was a fleet footed winger and all the Maori team laughed and their white teeth flashed and their chins and stomachs jiggled with good humour. "Well if you are a winger then what size of blokes are they who play in the forwards?"

More laughter ensued from this exchange and Bruce served the Rugby team with some Tooheys Flag Ale as the dozen lonely bottles of Stein Lager had long gone.

Bruce was a bit worried, "Jeez Jane they are drinking the beer pretty quickly I hope we don't run outta beer."

"Don't worry Bruce we can convert them to some of Australia's finest beers and in no time they will develop a thirst for Tooheys. Just mention Tooheys KB or a drop of Flag Ale and stand back and watch them go for it. I have never met a Kiwi to knock back a cold beer," and Jane wandered off to her place in the back office to sort out some paperwork.

No doubt about Jane, she could always see a way of overcoming any problem and Bruce was growing to depend on her more and more the longer he knew her.

"Jeez what a corker, the whole place would collapse without her," said Bruce as he turned and watched the lovely back of his sweetheart disappear from view.

Bill the barman called Bruce over and said to him, "Now Bruce, don't forget what the boss said about the thief who is snitching drinks from the bottles and not paying for it. Now we have a pretty good idea who it is and that one armed cleaner seems to be a bit slow in doing his work. In other words he has a load aboard before he starts work and gets worse as the day gets longer."

"Yes and don't forget whoever it is may be getting into the guest's rooms and sleeps in their beds. If it is Flipper the cleaner then why don't we just front him and tell him to stop?"

"We could do that but the boss wants me to put pencil marks on the labels tonight when we close up, the only person who will be here will be our one armed friend. In the morning we can check the levels of the grog bottles and if they have dropped then we've got him."

Bruce nodded and said, "You're right, we have got to be sure before we open our mouths. There are a few weird characters around here that's for sure."

"We certainly do I could talk all day and part of the next about some of the mob that come in here," laughed Bill as he rolled his eyes and lifted his hands in prayer.

"Did I ever tell you about the local mailman? Well Postie was in here drinking away all morning and still hadn't started work. He just wanted one more beer didn't he and after he had that one we reminded him again that he should get moving and deliver the mail, but the poor sod said that all would be jake and he just wanted one more beer for the road."

"Eventually we all prevailed upon him to finish up his beer and get off his stool and start work. However, while all this was going on good old Chalky had smeared his spectacles with boot polish or somethin' so old postie was blind in more ways than one when he left here to do his rounds."

20

Bruce laughed and said, "That would do it, and what happened then?"

"Postie got in his utility truck and off he went in first gear with the engine screaming. And as the story goes he was driving along the street and steering through a bit of a haze when he saw a turn off and swung the ute onto the new road. He crept around the road at a respectable ten miles per hour, still in first gear and came to a gap in the fence and chucked one of the mailbags out and continued on his way. He motored on through the haze of smeared glasses and too many beers for a while and then saw a mail bag lying on the side of the road to be collected, so he stopped and picked it up and threw it in the back and then drove on.

"Yeh, that sounds OK, glad the old codger was doing his postman's job," laughed Bruce.

Bill continued the story, "Well the problem was that Postie had driven onto the Randwick Race Course and was going round and around the race track and that mailbag was being thrown out of the ute and on the next lap picked up and this went on until Postie got tired. The poor old bloke never did get his mail delivered that day."

"Amazing, no wonder the post office gets a bit of a thrashing about the mail being late, what happened then?" asked Bruce.

"Well, one of the race course attendants found him asleep in the ute right in the middle of the race track near the finishing line and shook his shoulder. When Postie had woken up the attendant kindly suggested that he gallop off and park his truck somewhere else."

Bruce laughed and pulled a beer for one of the regulars in a blue singlet and said to Bill, "That is amazing, I wonder how he felt after all that beer?"

"Don't worry about that, worry about the poor blighters who were expecting their mail. To this day we are not sure that one of the mail bags is still not out there at Randwick Race Course with the grass growing around it."

Chapter 4

Bruce Cooks Brekkie

Bruce was making his way down the hotel's corridor to the door leading to the cellar as it was his turn for cellar duty. However, he paused at the head of the stairs when the bar manager called out to him.

"Hang on a minute Bruce can I see you for a sec?"

Smiley beckoned Bruce into his office and closed the door. "Have a seat lad".

"Owareyerz this mornin' Smiley?"

"Good oh mate, now Bruce I want to speak with you before you started downstairs today as I need you to help out in the kitchen. Cook has gone walkabout, most probably suffering from too many glasses of the cooking sherry again and we would like you to cook breakfast."

Bruce took in this bit of information and his face got a little bit redder but apart from him stopping breathing no one would have noticed. "Strike a light Smiley I can't cook to save me flamin' life."

"Now now Bruce it will be OK. I understand you have had a bit of experience up in the bush cooking breakfast and well we are desperate and we thought of you."

"Wot, you mean cook for all the hotel guests, I don't think I have that kind of experience, all I did was to help Jacko the cook a few times and all he would do was to yell at me. I know, I've a great idea, how about

Janie? She is a woman and ladies are good at that sort of thing."

"Ha, I will tell her you said that Bruce so you had better watch out! Anyhow you've had some experience out in the bush cooking for the drovers and well we need you to start like now as it's almost eight o'clock. Don't worry Bruce there are only a few guests who will be wanting a feed and they don't eat much. That shouldn't cause much of a problem to someone with all your experience."

Bruce thought to himself "Jeez it's not fair", but thought better of it and shook his head and muttered, "You've gotta be kiddin'... me, cook ... not if you don't want a whole lot of deaths on yer hands."

Smiley thought that was a great joke and his moustache twitched and his face almost broke into a grin, "Now off you go mate and give it your best shot. My suggestion is to keep it simple and why don't you just give 'em toast, tea, beans and grill a few sausages or something?"

Bruce sighed and got to his feet and wandered off to the kitchen, "Thanks a lot Smiley," came the voice as he faded away down the corridor to his doom.

Bruce stood there in the silent kitchen, except for a lone fly circling aimlessly. He breathed in and the usual hotel kitchen smell of stale food, cooking oil and garbage assaulted his delicate nostrils. It sure ponged and Bruce's stomach almost turned over. He shrugged, shook his head and found a list of who was staying at the Pub and worked out that he had four breakfasts to cater for and with banging and clattering lit the stove, started to boil the kettle and plugged in the toasters.

He pulled a tray of a dozen sausages out of the cold room, opened a few cans of baked beans and looked for the knife to cut up the round topped loaves of bread for the toast.

Bruce was going to chalk up the menu in the dining room and list the meals but put the chalk aside to do it later and started to hum a few bars of his favourite song, Personality.

While he was tipping the baked beans into a large saucepan and waiting for the stove to heat up Bruce failed to see that his other love, Greta the Alsatian dog had sidled into the kitchen.

Now like any red blooded dog Greta was no fool when it came to eating. Any hint of food brought her like a fly to a sheep and Greta's large nose had a few million scent buds or something housed there which made her a smelling machine on four legs.

Bruce was well into the second run through of his song as he hummed and whistled away when he turned to get the sausages for the grilling.

When he looked at the table he stopped in shock and his heart started beating at 500 beats per minute. "Jeez where have the flamin' snags got to?"

Instead of twelve sausages lying proudly on the plate Bruce saw that the plate was empty and the sausages had disappeared. Now there were three possibilities. One was that one of the lads was playing a trick, or there was a sausage loving ghost snooping around the pub or Jane's big friend Greta had snitched them.

Just to make sure that they had not slipped off the plate onto the floor, after all they could always be picked up and dusted off, nobody would know, Bruce knelt as if in prayer and gave a quick look around under the table and the surrounding floor. It soon dawned on him that the sausages had gone and in fact had gone for good and were destined never to return.

"Crikey, where have the dratted snags gorn, I'm for it now!" said Bruce as he straightened up and scratched his head.

It was then that his gaze fell on Greta sitting there in the corner with a funny look on her face. It could have been a smile.

"Now Greta old girl you couldn't have could yah? Nah you wouldn't do that to your old mate Brucie wouldja?"

Before Greta could answer in dog language Bruce's very best love entered the kitchen with a beaming smile on her face. Usually when he saw Jane his heart would lurch a little and he would always break into a smile. However, now the hotel breakfast had been sabotaged by a silly looking smelly dog; he could barely raise a smile.

"Hello Bruce, oh there you are Greta, What are you looking so glum about Bruce darling?" said Jane as she looked from Bruce's woebegone face to Greta's smiling sausage filled fat head.

"Er, Janie something terrible has happened I think that Greta is about to drop pups or she has just snaffled me dozen snags, jist look at the gut on 'er."

Jane turned to look at the bashful dog and could not help laughing. Sure enough the dog had a very swollen stomach, "Greta you naughty girl."

When Greta heard Jane call her a naughty girl she knew that she would escape being sent to the dog home. If a dog could smile then Greta was beaming as she thumped her tail and wagged away. Now if Jane had said we will grind you up into sausages then Greta would have shot through like a Bondi tram. All that was heard was a few thumps of Greta's tail on the floor.

"Jeez Jane, this is serious what am I going to do, I am in real trouble here as the guests will be wanting to eat their breakfast and ... well, breakfast has gorn!"

"Well let's not worry too much about it; we can offer them something different, it doesn't have to be sausages, we can always open a can or two."

"Crikey, Jane that's the ticket I can give 'em baked beans and toast; anyone can cook that and then with luck I will never have to work in the kitchen again."

Bruce set to with a will and whistled a few more bars of Personality cutting up the bread for toast while Jane dumped a few cans of Heinz best baked beans in a giant saucepan and started heating them up.

"Yeh that will do the trick, but I think that Greta should go outside Bruce with her tummy full of sausages I don't want her anywhere near the hotel for the next day or so. The results could be spectacular."

Just at that time the first guest arrived and plonked himself down at the first table that offered and looked over at the blank black board to see the menu. Seeing nothing on the board he then swung his head around and saw Bruce hovering there looking lost and assumed rightly that he was in charge of the sumptuous repast that the hotels are known for.

"What have you got on this morning young fellow?" Came the clipped tones of the English gentleman from room number four.

Bruce felt like saying, have a look at the menu you silly Pommie git, but as he had forgotten to chalk it up he just mumbled, "Er um, we've got baked beans on toast sir."

"Yes, well what else have you got?" enquired the toff from the old dart.

"Well we have baked beans, baked beans on toast and toast and that's pretty well it coz we had a disaster in the kitchen."

The gentleman from England was silent as he took in the news that there was no sausages or bacon and eggs, a typical English breakfast, and knew that all the tales his colleagues had told him about the Wild West, that is Australia, was true. Horribly true.

"But I'm hungry, real hungry, surely you've got more than that, what else have you got," said the Pommie in the fruity accents of Oxford.

"Well we have nuffink really just beans I reckon coz we had a disaster in the flamin' kitchen," said Bruce firmly looking the man right in the eye.

"Beans what sort of beans?" said the obviously hungry and disbelieving new comer to Australia's fair shores.

"Mister, I told you we got beans on toast or beans by 'em selves and that's all we've got," said Bruce fast losing his patience with the obviously dim-witted and mentally challenged tourist.

The hungry guest by now the centre of attention as a few more hotel guests had entered the dining room, thought for a while and said, "Well my good man I don't like beans and I don't like beans on toast either, so there."

"Well in that case you could have toast and jam and a cuppa tea, how does that sound mate?" Said Bruce smiling with his flash of brilliant menu creativity.

"I don't like jam what else have you got?" replied the Englishman who by this time was really not one of Bruce's favourite people.

Bruce spoke through gritted teeth, "Now look here Mister, we have flamin' baked beans and we got bloody baked beans and toast so what are you goin' to have?"

Jane had materialised and was standing there looking at the heavy breathing and red faced Bruce and saw the red face and staring eyes of the hotel guest and thought it would be a good idea to defuse the situation before Bruce resorted to type and donged the Pommie on his scone.

Baked beans graced the plate of the Pommie and sat there steaming away.

"Mr. Campbell-Smythe we don't have anything else this morning I'm afraid, we will rustle up a plate of the best baked beans ever created and lovely wholemeal toast with good Australian butter for you so how about that?"

The red faced man from England, never used to be told no by a mere Colonial, at last gave in as he knew that if he wanted something to eat it had better be baked beans, said to Jane, "Well in that case I will have beans on toast, thank you young lady."

Bruce and Jane disappeared into the kitchen and in no time had returned with a plate of beans for the man.

"That will fix yer up mate," said Bruce as he thumped the plate on the table and shot through back to the safety of the kitchen.

The Englishman looked at the black board with no meals shown, stared at his plate of baked beans and glared at Bruce's retreating back before shrugging his narrow shoulders and picked up his knife and fork and attacked his breakfast ravenously.

"How did it go Bruce, did Mr Campbell-Smythe look a bit happier when you served him?"

"Nah he still looked kinda drippy but I reckon all Pommies must look like that. I hope that cook surfaces tomorrow I would not like to go through all this again. I reckon we should hide the cooking sherry from her though."

Bruce spoke to the large dog who was looking very pleased with herself, "Greta old girl I reckon you will get no dinner tonight even if you have not digested all the sausages you scoffed."

Jane laughed and called for the rotund Greta and drifted off to the office to move some paper around and Bruce started serving up another three plates of baked beans and toast to the other guests.

A few whistled bars of the song 'Personality' plus the clattering of pots and pans could be heard from the kitchen as Bruce served up another plate of beans.

Chapter 5

Barry the Bard

B ruce had arrived at the Auckland Hotel just as it was being opened by Jane's father who was also up bright and early that morning.

"Good day to you Bruce, you are looking chipper today and what a day it is too."

"Yes, sir, it is alright and it is so good I stopped on the way here to have a look at the surf. It was beautiful and rolling in just nicely. There were the usual blokes out there surfing, lucky dogs."

The boss nodded and said, "Well Bruce I just wonder who the fellows are doing the surfing on a weekday. They must be either taking a sickie, out of work or wagging school."

Bruce laughed and said, "Lucky dogs."

The two men turned from the bright sun shine and entered the gloom and the odour of stale beer and cigarette smoke in the main bar. Bruce walked around turning on the lights and the boss returned a few stools to their correct place by the wall.

"Alright Bruce this morning I wonder of you could dust down the glass in the frames out the front here and when you have finished that come and see the manager as he may have some more jobs for you."

"Okeydokey," said Bruce as he started whistling his theme song.

Bruce was obviously enjoying his job at the hotel in Bondi as trainee hotel manager. Being close to his beloved Bondi Beach was a bonus and he couldn't wait until closing time so he could whiz down to the beach, dive in and do a bit of body surfing.

Hotels are known for always having something interesting going on and the Auckland Hotel was no exception. Bruce always wondered though about the name of the hotel until it was explained to him. He was told that when Jane's father bought the place he noticed there were thousands of New Zealanders living close by who had taken advantage of the short trip across the Tasman Sea to a land with warmer weather. Therefore, to attract their custom it was an easy step to just change the name of the hotel. By naming it after the largest city in the country it did not fail to draw them in and beer sales had skyrocketed.

Hotels seem to attract many different types. The locals, the workers, the eccentrics and the steady drinkers all claimed the Auckland Hotel as their second home.

Of course the tourists were a growing number too and many would enter the main bar to whet their whistle as they all had heard about the most famous beach in the world, Bondi. The first beach in the world to introduce life savers. Mind you the tourists often stayed for more than one beer and each one of them had their own story.

The locals were a colourful lot also and sometimes when it was quiet and there was not a lot of customers, Bruce would prop his elbows on the bar for a breather and slowly look around the bar to see who was there. He amused himself by trying to work out who they were and what their story was. In the gloom in the corner at the back was a bald heavy fellow with his head in the newspaper reading away.

"Who's that bloke over in the corner reading the paper Bill?"

"Oh, he's not reading the paper Bruce he is looking at the horse racing news in the sports section. That's Sammy the SP Bookie who will place your bets for you on the horses, the trots and the dogs."

"Alright then I will steer clear of him, so who is that over there near the window have you seen him before? The bloke looking kind of droopy and sad."

"Well Bruce I am not sure but I think that is the local undertaker and I suppose he looks like that all the time anyhow keep away from him unless you're dead or he wants another beer," smiled Bill.

"There are some funny people that come in here Bill, mind you up at Booleroo there were some strange fellows living around there too. You should have seen Jacko the cook a huge bloke over six feet six inches in his socks, if he owned any, and he was pretty big around his middle too. He was the cook and everyone was scared of him. In fact he terrified me."

"Is that where you got your experience in cooking baked beans from Bruce?"

"Yeh, kind of but I only helped out a few times when cooks helper had shot through. All of his helpers were an odd lot or else they would not have worked with him, coz he was a real fright! Every month or so they would take off and we would have to find another assistant for him."

"What did he do?"

"Well, he would scream at them if they had done anything to make him unhappy, and he was always unhappy. Believe me when that monster screamed at you then you had a cause to be scared because he was terrifying and most probably a mass murderer. He would throw things at you and smash things up and put his fist through the wall. It was horrible."

"Oh, come on Bruce."

"Well, OK he was not a mass murderer, but he could have been!"

"Now Bill let's change the subject from Jacko, he still gives me nightmares. Who is that little chap over there reading a text book?"

"Oh, he is one of the regulars. That text book is most probably one that he has written himself. He is a Professor, Barry the Bard, we call him, and he lectures on literature at Sydney University and he is a quiet gentleman until he has a few beers and then he undergoes a change."

The little man was obviously an intellectual. A furry sports coat, with leather buttons and leather patches on the elbows marked him as a man who lived in the halls of learning. He was a little under five foot six inches and his sparse hair was brushed back over a high forehead which no doubt had the space for a large brain.

Barry the Bard was indeed a poet for that puny frame and unprepossessing appearance had a deep but pleasant bass voice which held all those present enthralled. When he had more than a few beers he would start to recite poetry and what he loved to do was to give a Banjo Patterson recital. Barry could recite most of the poems of the greats like Henry Lawson, Dorothy Mackellar and the great Banjo Patterson but his favourite was the Man from Snowy River and some of the wags would give him a penny for every stanza he could remember.

Porky, one of the regulars, reckoned that the daft bugger was making the poems up as he was going along, but Bruce assured him it was the real thing. Not that Bruce would know because he left school early and escaped to go bush, reading books was not on the top of his to do list.

"Nah he is the full bottle alright when it comes to poems, like." Drawled a drinker in a three piece suit with a cardboard suitcase at his feet.

Because Bruce had asked about the poet the regulars, ever ready to have some entertainment all gathered around the Bard and helped him to clamber up onto the bar, to the whistles and cheers of the gathering crowd.

The Bard sipped a beer and then opened his mouth to speak. It only took the few opening lines of his favourite poem to bring a hush to all the chatter from the drinkers. Even though the lads would say they did not like poetry, all present would stop talking and start to listen and thrill at the great voice rolling over them.

A hush had descended on the patrons of the hotel as they heard,

"There was movement at the station, for the word had passed around

That the colt from old Regret had got away,

And had joined the wild bush horses—he was worth a thousand pound,

So all the cracks had gathered to the fray. "

And so it went on stanza after stanza until the Bard had finished and the whole place erupted in cheers and whistles.

Bruce was pleased to hear the great poem that the Bard had recited in such an exciting way and thought that there may be something to the idea of learning and reading books. That thought was quickly forgotten though when the Bard began to wobble and Bruce thought it may be a good idea to get him down before he hurt himself.

Barry the Bard stood there and sprouted his poetry.

It was always easier said than done and there was usually a problem how to encourage the Bard to come on down off the bar and be relegated to the ranks. If he was still standing the Bard would continue to sprout more and more poetry until somebody would grab him and pull him down before he fell down.

After fifteen minutes of poems Bruce thought that the time had come to step in and stop any damage to the Professor. The Bard was by this time wobbling alarmingly and the once great voice had started to mumble a little, he had even started to sniffle at the passages of a sad poem.

Looking up at the little man Bruce called out, "Come on down now Professor there is a good fellow."

The Bard who was standing there murmuring some bush ballads wiped a tear from his eye and two of the regulars helped Bruce get the poet down from the bar.

"There, there Professor, cheer up mate, how about we get you another beer and you can have a packet of Smiths Chips on the house, whadderya say about that?" as Bruce gently patted the Bard on the back and ushered him over to a seat in the corner.

"You are too kind my dear fellow," slurred the Bard as Bruce walked off to get the beer and chips.

In the meantime the poet of Bondi had started sprouting a few more lines of verse to the two workers in blue singlets at the next table who were not sure if he was speaking English.

Chapter 6

The Ladies Saloon Bar

Bruce was getting the hang of his job and mixing drinks and pouring beers was easy, what was hard was dealing with the many customers of the pub, they all had their little quirks and likes and dislikes.

Just before lunch Smiley asked Bruce to take the fully laden drinks tray into the ladies lounge down the hall. Bruce set off and soon heard the hub bub as he neared the saloon door. His heart beat a little faster as he was a little fearful as to what lurked behind the frosted glass swinging doors.

"Gulp I am for it now," said Bruce as he swallowed and his Adams apple bobbed nervously.

The sounds of high pitched laughter and many voices raised in conversation suddenly became quieter as the door swung open with the aid of Bruce's foot. The smell hit Bruce's nose. Cigarettes, stale perfume and beer did not make a heady mix. He kept the door open with his rear end as he set himself and then wobbled into the Ladies Lounge holding the tray of drinks.

There were a few giggles from up the back but the crowd of red faced old dames waited expecting the new waiter to drop the lot. Bruce struggled to keep himself upright and stop wobbling as he shuffled slowly forward. There was a hush as all the voices gradually stopped and Bruce felt himself go red and start to perspire. He concentrated and slowly, ever so slowly he made his way to the tables fearful that

38

the tray of full glasses would jiggle too loudly and even topple over.

"Please God don't let me drop the flamin' thing," prayed Bruce under his breath.

The scuffle of his shoes on the carpet, the tinkling of the ice cubes in the glasses, the rattle of the bottles against each other, all could be heard in the hushed silence. At last his horrible snail paced journey was at an end and he thankfully arrived at the first table. When he stopped at the table a loud cheer erupted from the old dames and some even clapped.

Bruce's face went even redder.

"Here you are ladies 'Pims Number 1 Cup', a shandy and a gin and tonic for you."

The ladies smiled coyly up at Bruce while Bruce knowing he was being scrutinised by every old bag in the room managed to go a deeper shade of red.

He then turned to totter over to the next table which was occupied by an even older lady who was decidedly frisky after a few 'G and T's'.

"Oh you have my gin and tonic with a slice of lemon young man," simpered Mrs. Potter the lady with the fluffy yellowy white hair as she gave Bruce what she thought was one of her most endearing smiles. Unhappily for her the effect was lost on Bruce as he was concentrating so much to make sure the drinks did not spill that he missed the teeth stained by red lipstick smile from the lady.

Now Mrs. Potter may have been a pretty girl or a lovely bride or even matured into a beautiful woman but since then more than a few decades or more had fled and the old darling's beauty had long faded behind the layers of makeup and beneath the curly wig.

Bruce tottered over to the lady and the tray wobbled alarmingly

She was a kind old dame but as with many of the old girls they were interested to see Bruce the new lad working at the pub. They may have had daughters which he could be introduced to or something and they certainly were interested to learn if he had a steady girl-friend.

With her eye lashes fluttering alarmingly, to the extent that Bruce thought that there was something wrong with the old girl's eyes or she was going to keel over in a faint, Mrs. Potter said "Tell me young man do you have a girl-friend, you know someone special to love?"

Blimey thought Bruce, "Now I'm for it ...... yeh, I sure do Mrs. Potter," mumbled Bruce trying to keep his voice down so none of the other ladies would hear what he said.

"Can't hear you young man," shouted Mrs. Potter who was inclined to be deaf and had by this time put her hand up to cup her ear, "Do you have a girlfriend?"

The whole Saloon had gone quiet again and Bruce knew he could not evade the question, so he raised his voice louder so the old dame could hear him.

"Yeh, I have a girl-friend all right and she's a corker."

Dead silence reigned and then all the old girls cheered and clapped again. If faces could get redder then the world had not witnessed any redder than poor Bruce's, he was so embarrassed. The old dames had made him feel more than uncomfortable. It would be easy for him to turn around and take to his heels but a matter of pride made him stay and face the music. Just as well he was not a wicked person otherwise he could have mixed up some real nasty cocktails for the old bags. However, if they did not leave him alone he may forget he was a good bloke.

He looked around him and saw some of the old girls at the other tables and one in the corner sipping on her cup of tea while she was knitting bootees or something in a garish bilious yellow. Like something that Greta the dog had eaten and spat out. Give him the main bar where the clientele were the men of Bondi, sportsmen, working types and tourists.

By late afternoon Bruce had enough of the ladies in the Saloon Bar. He had improved his rate of mixing the drinks and delivering them and he felt that he was getting pretty good at all that but what he was not coping with was the smart aleck comments from the fair damsels of Bondi.

Every time he entered the Saloon carrying a tray to set down the drinks, packets of Smiths Chips and collect the empty glasses to take back to the bar he was subjected to silly and teasing comments from the old girls.

"Crikey, they all reckon they are comedians, I will make sure I get to miss serving this lot in future, they are worse than a mob of silly galahs when they bring the wheat in."

On returning to the bar Smiley called to Bruce and asked him to stay back after closing time at 6 o'clock for a staff meeting. At the appointed hour Bruce gathered with all the hotel employees and saw that Jane's father, the owner of the hotel, was there too.

The owner of the hotel said in a loud voice, "Alright ladies and gentlemen, I need to let you know that we have a cat burglar in the hotel. The culprit has been drinking from the bottles and has been entering the guest's rooms and sleeping in their beds. I would like you all to keep a look out for anyone who looks suspicious and see the Manager, Mr. Cavalier."

Everybody started talking at once as a little bit of excitement was rare in the hotel and everyone was enjoying the idea that they could apprehend the thief and relieve the boredom.

Comments could be heard such as, "I wonder who it could be, have you seen anyone around here that looks suspicious. I will jump on the bugger and give 'im a good pounding. It could be one of us."

The next day Bruce was leaning against the bar after pulling a few beers and idly watching Flipper the hotel's old one armed cleaner who was sitting in a corner drinking a gin.

"You know Bill I wonder if Flipper is the cat burglar he gets stuck into the gin and does not do a lot of cleaning around here, that's for sure."

"Yes Bruce, nothing would surprise me, after all whenever Flipper is at work he seems to be wobbling a bit and disappears for long periods of time. He certainly does not seem to be doing much cleaning. I have always wondered how a one armed cleaner can use a broom, mind you I've never seen him use it."

The two friends looked over the room to where the one armed cleaner was downing his gin and then looked at each other with broad grins on their faces.

"Are you goin' to tell Smiley or will I?" asked Bruce.

"Nah, I reckon the poor old coot needs his rest," said Bill as he served another regular with a middy of new.

Chapter 7

Hey, it's the Sallies

Bruce was whistling his theme song again...
'Personality,' by the US singer Lloyd Price was
his favourite song and he always believed that
he had plenty of personality so Bruce thought he
deserved his own theme song.

Personality trailed away into silence, well almost
silence, as Bruce heard a terrible banging, thumping
and squealing coming from outside the hotel. The
noise was terrible. Jane's headache was not being
improved either by the deep booming of the base
drum that was reverberating off the tiled floor and
bare walls of the bar.

"Crikey and stone the flamin' crows what is that
racket?" Shouted Bruce to make his voice heard
above the noise from outside.

"Yeh, close the bloody doors and windows or
somethin'," yelled one of the regulars who then put
his fingers in his ears to cut down on the noise.

Smiley the Manager stuck his head out of the office
door and yelled, "Yeh, go on out there Bruce and tell
them to pipe down or something, the noise is coming
straight in the doors and if they keep it up then all the
regulars will go to the Bondi Arms Hotel down the
road and we will all be looking for a new job comes
Monday!"

Bruce made sure the cash register was closed, as
he could not face it if the takings were pilfered. He
drifted over to the doors to shoulder his way through

the regulars and see what the commotion was about. He peered out the doors of the pub and saw before him a group of uniformed people, like a ring of black crows, who were the Salvation Army band of Bondi, in full swing banging away and looking holy.

Bruce was serving a beer when he heard an awful racket

All the regulars had stopped their talk and more importantly, their drinking of Mr. Toohey's finest brew, and were peering through the pub's windows and hanging out the doors looking at the entertainment outside. The red faced lot of regulars were yelling in various degrees of inebriation varying from encouragement to bordering on the rude like ....." good on yer, you're a beaut sheila, garn, getoutavit and couldn't play a tune to save yer life."

Bruce heard one of the wags say with a hoot of laughter "the boys will find any excuse to have some fun."

"Any excuse for fun! Jeez they're hard up for entertainment if they want to go and listen to that lot," yelled Bruce over the tootling of the band leader's trumpet.

The noise continued and the deep booming of the base drum and the screeching of the brass plus the ribald yells and comments from the patrons made a din that became impossible to think.

The Sallies were in a circle and looking pretty serious as they blasted away with 'Onward Christian Soldiers' while the prettiest of their number, a fetching young sweetie with no makeup to grace her lovely face and her hair pulled back severely under her bonnet, passed around the red bucket for donations to the needy.

The trumpeter was blowing for all he was worth and his face glistened with sweat. "Blat, Fflat."

The lady with the symbols was having a lovely time of it too and pity help anyone who got in the way of her swinging arms. "Crash, Blash"

The base drummer was entering into the fun of it all and was swinging the padded sticks for all he was worth. "Boom, Pfhoom."

The Sallies were at it again, and the noise was horrendous

And the ladies were singing away mightily while rattling away with their tambourines. "Clatter, Flatter."

There were even some of the old dames from the Saloon singing along with quavering voices. All of this added up to a mighty noise and everyone seemed to be having a good time.

There was one little kid who had a blue balloon on a string and was jumping up in the air trying to snare the trombone player's slide every-time the player pushed the slide out.

"Crikey what a racket," yelled Bruce to the lovely young woman who was shaking the red bucket in his face for a donation.

"Thank you sir, glad you like it we don't often get compliments on our music. I will ask them to give us another one, how about a rousing hymn to our Lord "Amazing Grace' followed by 'How Great Thou Art'?"

"Jeez, er OK, that would be the ticket," gulped Bruce and beat a hasty retreat before he ended up ordering a whole afternoon of hymns.

Retreating to the relative quiet of the empty bar Bruce went looking for Smiley and Jane but they seemed to have also abandoned ship and gone to look at the Sallies entertaining the population of Bondi.

In a few minutes the noise outside seemed to lessen and with a few final toots and squeals and rude shouted comments from the red faced brigade the Sallies must have moved off because everyone trooped back into the pub shouting and laughing. In no time Bruce was flat out like a lizard drinking pouring beers.

The bar was three deep with drinkers ordering their drinks. They were giving Bruce orders like, "Now how about the best of brews there's a good bloke, giveusah coldie mate, can I've a middy, two shandies there's a good chap and a lisping have you got a sweet sherry my good fellow from some swell in a tweed jacket. There was even a few Maoris from New Zealand who were about to do a Haka to show the regulars how the All Blacks start their footie matches.

Bruce straightened his back and wiped his forehead when there was a lull in the beer orders and shook his head and said, "Jeez it takes all types here at Bondi that's for sure".

Smiley appeared from where he had disappeared to and Bruce asked him why the Salvation Army played their music at the pub.

Smiley never smiled or even grinned but he answered Bruce's question, "Bruce every flamin' Saturday afternoon they turn up at the front of the pub and scare all the drinkers away. They play a few hymns and hope that the dreadful house of ill repute, the hotel, will stop serving alcohol and start serving orange juice and lemon squash. Mind you I enjoy their playing and rather look forward to them coming and they do a lot of good. When they are finished here they move on to the other hotels in Bondi and end up at the beach on the boardwalk where they let her rip."

"Jeez the bloke with the trumpet looked like he was gunna blow a gasket rather than a tune. His face was redder than mine when I had to go and serve a few trays in the Ladies Saloon.

And didja see that bloke with the bass drum he was enjoying himself and I reckon everyone here in the bar would have liked to have a hit or two on the drum themselves, wadderyah think?"

Smiley shrugged and nodded, "I would be one of them Bruce, that Bass drum looks a lot of fun and it makes a hellavah racket. I will be off for a while Bruce so hold the fort for me will you?"

"OK Smiley, nothing seems to be happening so it will be smooth sailing," smiled Bruce.

One of the features of hotel life is that many of the people who frequent the bars are people that one is privileged to meet. Some are interesting characters, some have strange ways about them but the ones that Bruce was always warned about were the ones who could not hold their liquor. These fellows and an occasional old girl from the Ladies' Saloon could cause trouble. The problems that arose were anything from loud and raucous singing, swearing to an occasional smack across the ear or a down and out brawl.

The hotel was peaceful that afternoon, after the Sallies had entertained everyone with their music and singing, when two of the drinkers got into an argument. Bruce was standing there leaning up against the bar thinking about cool waters and slow rolling waves when he heard shouting and a scuffle.

Over near the front windows, with the lovely view of the beach, were two of the regulars having a set-to. With a sinking heart Bruce knew he was for it and as he was the only one at that time on the staff who was in the bar it was up to him to try and reason with the fellows to stop their fighting and swearing just in case someone got hurt.

Bruce walked over to them and called out, "Stone the bloody crows fellas how about putting a cork in it!"

As far as it went that was Bruce's first attempt at breaking up the two who took absolutely no notice. By this time the two men were silent but straining to overcome the other's hold. The heavy drinker with the blue singlet seemed to be getting the upper-hand over the smaller chap who was trying to twist his head around to bite his larger opponent on the arm. Mind you the arm was around his neck and his face was getting redder and redder by the minute.

"Crikey, you blokes how about you give it a rest!" was Bruce's next attempt at being a world class referee of wrestling and international peacekeeper.

The man with the teeth, the biter, had by then managed to get a mouthful of his opponent's, Blue Singlet's hairy arm and an anguished yell startled all the drinkers in the bar, who until now had stood there with amused looks on their faces.

"Jeez, can't you stop it you two or I will havetah call the police," bleated our hero and man of action.

By now all the patrons of the Auckland Hotel had gathered around in a big circle and the ever enterprising Sammy the SP Bookie was organising bets as to who would be the victor. "C'mon place your bets boys came the bass voice of Sammy, I will give yah two to one on the little guy with the well-developed laughing gear."

The wrestlers had eventually ceased to stay upright and had progressed to rolling around on the tiled floor. It appeared as if they were getting their second wind because the wild thrashing and yelling of 'Blue Singlet' and the biter was louder than before.

"What an athlete, look at the way he is throwing himself around," yelled one wag who saw Blue Singlet doing various unscientific wrestling moves.

"Nah, you would do the same if you had someone chomping and biting you on the chin," said one of the drinkers waving his hand around urging on the wrestlers while making sure his other hand firmly held his schooner of Tooheys New.

Bruce looked around at the now large crowd of regulars all shouting encouragement to their respective champions. "Bloody hell boys stop encouraging them, how about you give me a help in breaking 'em up?"

"Yis, I will fix 'em for yiz Bro as soon as my bloke wins," came the slurred voice of Maurie the Maori who loomed over the throng.

Maurie as you will remember was a huge man and all those standing near him had given him a wide birth, because if they were hit by one of Maurie's swinging ham like arms they would be in St. Vincent's Hospital in no time. You see Maurie was barracking for 'Blue

Singlet' who was by now sitting on chomper's head and had him in a toe hold or something. The biter was screaming at the top of his voice because his shoe had come off and his toe was being twisted until it looked like it was a cork being twisted out of a wine bottle.

Shouting to make himself heard above the shouts of the patrons urging their champions on, Bruce tried to make himself heard, "Jeez come on Maurie I have gotta get this under control or these blokes will get hurt or they'll smash something. Give me a hand."

Maurie the Maori's "Yis Bro" was lost in the cacophony of noise as the shouts and yells were echoing off the tiled floor and bare walls. Maurie effortlessly bent down and picked up the two men fighting and pulled them apart, like pulling burs off a blanket, and shook them to make them stop clawing and scratching to get at each other. Eventually the two dishevelled men ceased their struggles and looked up at the mountainous Maori.

"What didja do that fer, git orf me?" came the slurred voice of Blue Singlet.

The equally slurred voice of the man with the well-developed biting equipment said, "Yeh, leave 'im alone coz he's my mate, all we wuz doin' wuz havin' an argument about who pays the next round of drinks."

Maurie could not believe what he had heard and promptly dropped the two friends who subsided to the floor where they lay there with silly looks on their faces. Maurie shook his head and moved off back to the bar as the two wrestlers clambered to their feet and dusted themselves off. They then linked arms and supported each other as they meandered back to the bar for a couple of schooners of beer.

Wondering at the silliness of men who until a few moments before were for all intent of purposes trying to wreak homicide on each other, Maurie and Bruce watched the two drinkers happily down their beers in one long swallow. They then turned as one and unsteadily the best of friends wobbled their way to the double doors of the bar, waved a cheery goodbye to all and then disappeared from view.

"Thanks Maurie for helping there mate, that could have become dangerous."

"Yis, no problem Bro but they were more fun than the Salvation Army band and their singin' weren't they?"

The bar had quietened by now and had returned to a more serious subject which was the downing of as many beers as possible before closing time. By now Sammy the SP Bookie had paid out the winning bets and it looked like he had cleaned up as usual because he had shouted beers all round to his mates over in the corner.

As usual Smiley had arrived after all the ruckus and looked at his watch, "Oh, well it's close to six o'clock Bruce so start yelling time please gentlemen and get them to finish up so I can go home to my Missus."

Bruce raised his eyebrows and nodded thinking; "how does Smiley do it, he never seemed to be around when you needed him."

It took a quarter of an hour to clear the bar and after all the drinkers had been turfed out and the hotel was quiet all the lights were turned off and it was time for Bruce to meet up with Jane and walk home together. On the way out of the hotel Jane locked up and the local paper boy who was always on the corner outside the pub yelled "Paperrrz, do you want a Mirror or the Sun mate?"

Bruce stopped and paid his threepence for the Daily Mirror and folded it and caught up with Jane who had walked on further with her shadow Greta who had her nose down and her tail pointing in the air sniffing at anything that smelled interesting.

"You've bought the Mirror Bruce, I didn't know you read the newspapers. Are you catching up on the politics or sport?"

Bruce looked a bit shamefaced and hung his head to ponder a reply to Jane's question and she said, "C'mon Bruce why did you buy the paper?"

"Well Jane if you must know I like the 'Bluey and Curley' in the comic section."

"That figures," said Jane with a laugh as she linked her arm in Bruce's as they walked on.

Chapter 8

Bluey and the Fish Shop

The two young people were strolling along enjoying the day not that far away from the beach at Bondi. They could hear the sound of the waves as they rolled in all the way from far off South America. Just looking at the bright blue sky devoid of any clouds, one could tell that Sydney was in for a beautiful day. The seagulls wheeling overhead were up to their usual pranks and also seemed to be enjoying the sparkling day.

Bruce and Jane had taken some time off from the pub that Saturday afternoon and decided to take Greta for a walk along the promenade overlooking the beach at Bondi.

Greta strained at the lead and every so often would look around to see if her beloved Jane and Bruce were following her. She sniffed and sniffed checking on all the doggie smells and gave an occasional half-hearted tug to see if she was free to chase some seagulls who strayed too close.

An ice cream vendor was set up with his back to the sea against the wall. Bruce and Jane stopped and bought three vanilla cones ice creams one for each of them. Mind you it did not take long for Greta to swallow her ice cream and start pleading with her eyes to have some of Jane and Bruce's icy treat.

They stopped for awhile and Bruce gazed out over the concrete wall at the surf rolling in and idly watched the surfers out the back who were catching waves.

He happened to cast his gaze downwards and just below him were a group of girls sunbathing.

They sat there looking at the view, "This is the life Janie old girl."

"Jeez wot an eyeful of the sheilas, I was dreaming of this up on Booleroo Sheep Station for a few years and now I'm here, what a great life," mused Bruce to himself.

Jane caught Bruce's gaze and without a word gave him a not too gentle dig in the ribs from her very hard elbow, which occasioned Bruce to lift his gaze to the skyline and exclaim, "What a beaut view." Which earned him another but harder dig in the ribs.

"Greta really loved that ice cream Jane, it didn't touch the sides as it disappeared," said Bruce hoping to stop Jane reading his mind and thus avoid another sledge hammer blow to the ribs.

"Say how about we go around to the fish shop and get some fish and chips for lunch, we can also see dopey old Bluey who is working there."

"That sounds good but who is Bluey, I can't remember you mentioning him?"

"Well when I was out at Booleroo one of the drovers was Bluey and we were not great mates really but I would like to go and say gidday now that he lives down here in Sydney and works so close to us."

The three walked a block or so until they came to the fish shop. They peered through the grimy window into the dim recesses of the establishment and the first person they saw was Bluey clad in an apron and with a silly hat on his ginger head.

"Get a load of that willya there's good old Bluey slaving away, what a change we could never get him to raise a finger. The only time we had any excitement with Bluey was when he got lost in the paddock and we all had to go and look for him."

"Well it seems that you found him alright because there he is!" laughed Jane.

"Old Bluey was a pain in the butt alright and I bet he hasn't improved. Let's go in."

"I suppose I had better leave Greta outside as being so close to food she may do something that would embarrass us all. I still remember the cause of a peculiar breakfast being served at the hotel one morning when the sausages disappeared."

"Woof", barked Greta when she heard the word sausages.

"She is like you Bruce, loves sausages."

"Yep, I reckon the best meal in the world Jane is six sausages on a plate with mash potatoes and brown gravy."

The two young people ventured into the dim interior of the shop and paused there until their eyes grew accustomed to the light. Or rather the lack of it. The place ponged of fish, stale oil used for frying chips and a host of other smells which could not be readily identified.

They saw that Bluey was clasping a large orange fish to his chest which was so slippery that Bluey was having difficulty from dropping it on the floor.

"Gidday Bluey, looks like you've got a member of the family there."

Splat went the fish as it hit the floor.

"Ow, bugger me," yelled Bluey as he looked down at the huge slimy fish lying there in the dust and dirt.

"Look wot you've done, you've made me drop the flaming thing!"

It only took a second until Bluey realised that he recognised his fellow drover from the days out at Enngonia in the west of New South Wales.

"Oh hello Brucie wot you doing here?"

"Came to see you Bluey and the member of your family that you just dropped on the floor."

"Ah, very funny mate," said Bluey as he bent down and lifted the fish off the grimy floor. He wiped a few bits of fluff and dirt off its side with the end of his dirty apron and then laid it down on a bed of ice in the display cabinet.

Bluey, obviously very shy around the fair sex, was introduced to Jane and managed to blush a redder tint of red and hung his head as he said gidday. Jane smiled and raised her eyebrows to Bruce but did not say much.

Looks like you've got a member of your family there Bluey

The two ex-drovers spoke for a while about some of their friends still working with the sheep and Bruce realised that he did not have a lot to say to Bluey, in fact he never did. Bluey was a different species of mankind perhaps half man and half cave man or something. Definitely something that was a throwback to ancient man when he was still living in caves. He never had any conversation and did not have any favourite subjects. In fact he was one of those people who was very hard to speak with.

Jane could see that the conversation was sputtering to a close and took the opportunity to order fish and chips for two.

"Right you are cobber," said Bluey who brightened up with that and in no time pieces of fish and potato chips were frying away.

Thankfully it was soon time for them to say their goodbyes to Bluey. As a passing comment Bruce mentioned that Bluey would always be welcome at the hotel for a drink and then they thankfully they escaped the smelly confines of the fish shop into the sunshine.

"You know Jane, Bluey is better off down here by the beach and working in the fish shop, I reckon he will be happier here, and he may even find himself a girl. He certainly was not much chop as a drover. He lost himself and lost the sheep. They never did find his horse"

"What, he lost his horse?"

"Nah, just joking but he might have," laughed Bruce.

"Possibly Bruce, they say that there is somebody for everyone in this world, but Bluey may have to spend a lot of time looking for her."

"Yeh, too true Janie old girl, Bluey is always a little hard to take in big doses. Now let's go and tuck into the fish and chips coz Greta is starting to look hungry again."

Chapter 9

Stuck in the Bath

The hotel manager Mr. Valentine, also known as Smiley to the staff, came into the bar and beckoned Bruce and Bill the bartender over for a chat.

"Now fellows, you will remember we have had a problem with someone knocking off the grog out of the bottles of a night and also sneaking into guest's rooms and sleeping in their beds."

"Yeh, Smiley," said Bill and Bruce also nodded that he remembered to.

"Jeez Smiley, it wasn't me, coz if I'm tired I go home to me Mum and Dad's place for a lie down," said Bruce.

"Yes me either, I don't drink gin," said Bill.

"Settle down boys, listen we have been able to catch the person responsible, and we also had our suspicions for some time as to who it was. As you know we have been marking the bottles of a night at closing time and in the morning the level of the grog was always lower especially after the one armed cleaner had been on duty," said Smiley.

"Yes, I thought it might have been Flipper, there was not a lot of choice really," said Bill.

Smiley held his hand up for silence, "Well fellows I spoke with Flipper, I mean the cleaner, and we have agreed to part our ways and he has left to seek a job elsewhere."

"Golly, I hope the poor coot gets some work," said Bruce who was a kind hearted soul.

"At least we won't have to order so much gin now and the bar will show a bigger profit," said Smiley as he waved and walked back to the office leaving the two friends alone at the bar.

Bruce stood there leaning against the bar. His mind drifted off back to when he was a Jackeroo out west on the sheep station. Crikey it's hot and he decided to cool off. He stripped and threw his gear off as quickly as he could and dived into the dam. After the first shock of going under the muddy water Bruce realised he was only day-dreaming. He was no longer in Enngonia on Booleroo sheep station he was back where he belonged at his beloved Bondi just near the famous beach.

"Phew gasped Bruce just as well I was dreamin' coz I know where I would rather be. The flamin' flies will miss me though," and chuckled to himself as he gave a wipe to the bar top.

"Hello, hello wot was that"?

Bruce had not misheard for faintly somewhere in the hotel there was a cry for help. He could not imagine what would be the trouble but he now knew after a few months of working at the pub that there was always something happening.

The mixture of Bondi characters and alcohol seemed to bring about some really peculiar episodes and Bruce had quickly gained experience in handling what was thrown at him.

There it was again, a faint help, "Get me out of here", came floating down the stairs and along the hall.

The figure of Smiley the cellar manager appeared and he wildly looked around. "Gidday Bruce, do you hear it, it sounds like someone's in trouble."

"Yep, it does Smiley and it sounds as if it's coming from upstairs, let's get cracking and have a looksee".

The two men ran quickly along the hall and up the stairs where they stopped panting on the landing.

"Jeez there it is again and it sounds like Mrs. Greatley and it seems to be coming from the bathroom down the hall."

"Help, can anyone hear me?"

Smiley knocked on the door timidly, "Can we help Mrs. Greatley, are you alright?"

"No I'm not alright, I'm in the bath and I can't get out, help me," came the wailing reply.

Smiley looked at Bruce and Bruce looked at Smiley.

"Well Bruce I will leave it to you mate because I have a big day today down in the cellar and I need to ....," and Smiley shot through leaving Bruce gaping at the empty hall where until a few seconds ago his ex-friend and hotel manager was standing.

"Help, willya help me?" came the exasperated voice from behind the door.

Bruce knocked again and Mrs. Greatley yelled, "Will you stop floundering around out there and get in here and help me but don't look coz I'm in the bath and I'm stuck."

Bruce gulped at this news and slowly opened the door. Imagine his shock to see the guest and boy was she a big'un.

A big red face topped by curls was glaring at him, "Well don't just stand there do something. Just come over here and pull me out coz I'm stuck."

Bruce put his head down and shielded his eyes and almost tripped over the lady's slippers as he made his way to the bath. Boy she was a big one alright, must weigh a ton and she's covered in soap suds too. She will be hard to lift. The old gal looked like one of those pink ladies that old Macca, from the main bar, was always talking about. Macca loved large pink ladies. He reckoned there was more to cuddle. Skinny dames were not for Macca.

"Modern girls are just bags of bones mate, give me a bigun anytime," Macca would say out of a mouth that was missing a few teeth.

"Jeez, Mrs. Greatley how am I going to get you outta there, you're stuck?" whined Bruce while he was thinking that those soap suds are going to make it harder to pull the old girl out, she's going to be a bit slippery.

"That's a damn silly thing to say, I already told you that and don't just stand there grab my arms and pull."

The lady lifted up her arms and waved them at Bruce who cringed as if he was going to be hit.

The lady was getting redder in the face and her eyes were looking kind of mean, "For goodness sake what is wrong with you? Just get me out of here and don't you dare tell anyone what you've seen."

Bruce grabbed a slippery arm and gave a mighty heave but with no success. She did not budge and just sat there glowering up at him.

"Try harder!" she grated out between clenched teeth.

"Jeez lady I'm trying but I can't get a good grip onyer coz you're all slippery and how about I put my hand in and pull out the plug?"

"You mind where you put your hands, I've heard about your sort," said the lady with narrowed eyes as Bruce leaned over and felt around for the plug.

The lady's arm was kind of slippery, she was hard to budge that's for sure.

At last he felt it and it was quite hard doing all this with his eyes closed. He then pulled the plug and the water drained gurgling away. Leaving a horrible sight of a very large pink lady.

Bruce, who by now was soaking, closed his eyes again and then had a bright idea, "I know what to do Mrs. Greatley I will climb up on the end of the bath and grab yer arm and give it a good yank that may do it."

"Well get on with it then you stupid boy, I'm getting cold and anyone could walk in and see us. I've never been so embarrassed in all my life."

Clambering gingerly up onto the end of the bath, he balanced there precariously and grasped the lady's pink arm and pulled until he saw stars.

Well it was one of those old deep baths and she was after all a big lady but eventually with a big pop, something gave and Mrs. Greatley rose in the bath and stepped out.

"I'm going to complain to the management about this, just you wait and see," snarled Mrs. Greatley with as much dignity as she could muster.

Bruce jumped down from the end of the bath and shielded his eyes because the sight of the large pink lady was like a horror movie. He then felt his way to the door to get out of the bathroom as quickly, as possibly, he had enough frights for the day.

"Crikey, it was as bad as getting off the mad cow in Enngonia," grizzled Bruce to himself.

While moving towards the door to escape from the bathroom and the angry woman he had his eyes tightly closed and his arms outstretched in front of him like a sleep walker; Bruce made a terrible mistake.

He must have turned the wrong way, after all he did have his eyes closed, and instead of grabbing hold of the door handle Bruce grabbed something else which just happened to be part of Mrs. Greatley's ample chest.

When Bruce felt what he had grabbed his eyes opened in shock and exclaimed, "Jeez sorry lady, I couldn't help it," and quickly pulled his hand away as if it was burned and hid it behind his back.

The lady just looked at Bruce and quivering with rage pointed to the door without a word and waited until Bruce regained his senses.

"Don't you think it is time you went somewhere else?" said Mrs. Greatley through gritted teeth.

"Yeh, sorry lady, gulp ....." Bruce fled from the bathroom and didn't even say hooroo or tattah to the lady and crash went the door as he slammed it shut and clattered down the stairs.

"Jeez she didn't even say thank you, some people can be so ungrateful," grumbled Bruce as he made his way down to the bar and safety.

On reaching the ground floor and breathing heavily Bruce entered the main bar and immediately all the drinkers in the place, who had been informed of Bruce's predicament by Smiley, were waiting for him. They all started cheering and clapping.

"Good on yer Brucie what a champion!" came the chorus of shouts and whistles from the louts.

"Oh, you're my hero," lisped one of the drinkers and fluttered his eyelashes and blew him a kiss.

"Crikey, give me a break fellas you cannot possibly imagine what I have just been through," said Bruce rolling his eyes as he went off in search of a towel.

Chapter 10

Wullie the Wee Scott

It was a quiet afternoon in the main bar of the hotel. That morning Bruce had helped out in the cellar rolling some barrels of beer around, sorting some whisky, brandy, port wine and checked very carefully on the sweet sherry records to see that the cook had not knocked off any. Everyone knew that the dear old soul did not always use the sweet sherry for cooking and it accounted for her erratic disposition and slap dash meals.

Bruce's sweetheart Jane worked in the hotel's office and was in her quiet way very capable. Bruce on the other hand had quickly found that paperwork was not one of his strengths and he knew that all he had so far gained since he left school was not much use to anyone in running a hotel.

Being a Jackeroo on a sheep station in the west of the state where it was dry and hot was where Bruce had been. He did not see many people, except his mates he worked with and an occasional mob of kangaroos and the bunch of feral pigs down by the tank could not be counted either. Now that he had relocated to the big smoke he was back where he belonged, of that he was sure.

Living close to the beach where he could have a surf or just laze away floating on his back looking at the blue sky was his idea of heaven. Also catching a wave to shore, doing a bit of sun-bathing and sharing a couple of ice creams with Jane was pretty good too. He was a man of simple tastes and the simple carefree existence he lived in and around Bondi was perfect.

Later that afternoon Bruce was serving a few drinks for the regulars and Maurie the Maori and a few of his hulking Maori friends were leaning up against the bar.

"Gidday Maurie do you want another round of beers mate?"

The giant Maori footballer turned to his friend who was even bigger than he was and got the nod from his companion, "Yis, bro, set them up. We've already had a start on and Hori has bet us all that he can drink a beer faster than anyone in the pub."

All the gigantic Maoris grinned with mouths with missing teeth and bashed each other on the back in horse play. Bruce winced because if he was hit like that he would have ended up with a broken back and been carted off to the St. Vincents Hospital for a few months to straighten out.

"We would like pints of Tooheys New all 'round bro and you should hang around and watch Hori get beaten," came the gap toothed smile and slurred endorsement of Hori's drinking prowess, from one of the All Black footballers.

Five giant pint glasses were taken down from the shelf and Bruce sloshed the beer in and waited for the collar to settle down before he topped them up and slid the amber filled glasses over the counter to the footballers for their drinking contest.

"Aye, what a beauty," said one of the giants as he blew the foam off the top and got ready to tip it down his gullet.

All the customers by this time had gathered around the Maoris and were eagerly waiting for the contest to start. There were a few Aussies who decided they would join in as well so everyone agreed it would be an international competition.

Maurie was the self-appointed time keeper and had his watch in one giant paw and said at the top of his voice, "Alright Hori, get Ready, Sut, Go!"

The footballer raised his glass and opened his throat and poured the beer down to the chanting from the crowd that had gathered around them. "Down, down, down, down."

In no time the empty glass was bashed onto the counter and Hori stepped back with a wide smile as a small amount of froth still adhered to his pudding face.

Maurie yelled to the cheering bar flies, "You beudy, 4.5 seconds! Can anyone beat that?"

There were many takers and the competition continued with the Maoris taking on all comers. After a lot of spilt beer, yelling and verbal jousting from the Aussie and Kiwi drinkers Maurie, the official timekeeper declared the contest a draw.

"C'mon boys how about another round, so fell 'em up Brucie and we can have another go," yelled a very happy Maurie.

Bruce served up the beers and then turned away and noticed a forlorn figure slumped in a dark corner who he identified as one of the bar flies, one with the defining nick name of Stinker. On closer examination Stinker seemed to be all banged up.

Stinker had a pained look on his face, which had a few bruises and a scrape down his forehead that was still an angry red and the bruises looked fresh. Two black eyes and a missing front tooth completed the description of his visible injuries. He certainly looked a very sorry Stinker.

Bruce turned to the barman and pointed out the sad and sorry figure of Stinker sitting in the corner by the back door, "Crikey Bill, what happened to him he is all banged up and by the looks of him he should be in hospital not sucking on a beer in the pub?" said Bruce.

Bill a barman with many years of experience in observing the regulars at the hotel looked up at Bruce and then swung around to see who he was referring to and laughed ruefully.

"Ah I see what you mean, well Bruce one of the lads was telling me that after closing time last night Stinker, who was the worse for wear after downing countless schooners of Tooheys finest ale, staggered off home to his lodgings. Well he decided that it was a long way and he wasn't moving quickly enough so on the spur of the moment he decided to take a short cut. In doing so he hopped over someone's back fence and saw in the darkness their swimming pool. Well it was a hot night and Stinker felt like cooling off so he dived in didn't he?"

"Fair enough, I don't blame him, if he was hot, I've done that meself up on Booleroo sheep station coz it's so hot," said Bruce.

"Well mate, mind you no one bothered to tell Stinker that the owners had gone away and they had emptied the pool, no water in it at all. Stinker had a hard landing alright and luckily it was in the shallow end. If it was the deep end he would not be here but in hospital as you said. He told his mates that he lay there all night until daylight so when the sun rose so did good old Stinker. He used the pool stairs to clamber out and continue on his way home. As you can see he made it and bright and early he is back here to have a few more schooners for a top up, so he will not feel his aches and pains."

"Crikey Bill I think I'm sorry I asked, I will say nothing when he orders another schooner, I don't want to hear the gory bits," said Bruce as Bill wandered off to the other end of the long bar to pull a few more beers.

At that moment Stinker gave out a moan and then a hacking cough and no doubt the poor old chap had caught a cold lying out under the stars all night, at the bottom of the swimming pool. Stinker's missus no doubt would not have been pleased to know that the pool had no water in it. Or would she?

Bruce had often seen his fellow drovers the worse for wear suffering from the effects of too much alcohol, but poor old Stinker in the corner looked like he should be lying on a morgue's slab rather than propped up in the corner.

Bruce walked up the bar to join Bill and asked if he would like some help in polishing the glasses. While the two men were busy working away getting ready for the five o'clock rush Bill said, "You know Bruce that yarn about Stinker is one of many as the pub always has a few funny tales to tell."

"You see Frankie, he's over there with a couple of mates. Did you ever hear about him and the stray dog?"

"No you haven't told me that one"

"Well he arrives home from the pub with a few too many beers aboard and there sitting on his doorstep is a stray dog wagging his tail. Now Frankie boy is a dog lover but this dog was very persistent and wanted a pat or something and would not let him get into his house let alone open the flaming front door. Well

Frank was busting and in a hurry to go somewhere real fast as nature was calling so he pushed the dog away but it came back wagging its tail and jumping up at him, you know the usual doggie thing."

Bruce slid two Pint glasses over to the contestants

"Well good old Frank by this time was getting pretty desperate so he donged the dog on the noggin. Not hard mind you but he must have hit 'im harder than he thought coz he killed the poor thing."

"Nah, the poor doggie, what did he hit him with?" asked Bruce in disbelief.

"Yeh, well Frankie was so desperate to get into the house to answer the call of nature that he just grabbed the first thing that was handy and well it was a house brick which his missus had on the front doorstep to put notes under for the Milko."

"Gosh, what happened then?"

"Well Frankie picked up the body and struggled over to the garbage bin and put the dog in real gently."

"Oh, the poor dog what happened then?" and Bruce frowned and looked over with a skinny eyed look at Frank who was innocently sipping on his beer in the corner.

"Well two days later Frankie goes to put the rubbish out and lifts the lid and out jumps the dog, he, ah, er only knocked the poor flamin' thing out."

Bruce started to laugh and asked, "Did the dog stay around for a pat?"

"Nah, shot through like a Bondi tram that's what he did. Not seen him since."

Bill wandered off whistling and left Bruce to polish a few more middy glasses.

The days in the hotel at Bondi were always different. Bruce found that every day there was something interesting and he never knew what or who would walk in through the doors.

It was with some surprise though that he noticed the noisy group over in the corner had suddenly become quiet and were staring at two new figures standing at the bar waiting to place their orders.

Bruce looked around the beer taps and saw before him a tall gentleman clad in a suit with a fedora hat looking ill at ease and apparently very hot as he was perspiring noticeably. What did make the two figures something to stare at was the little boy standing beside the gentleman. He was dressed in highland regalia and his kilt was way down past his knees.

"What would you like to drink Mister?" said Bruce leaning over the bar to have a closer look at the little fellow who looked up at him with bright blue eyes in a serious face.

The man brightened visibly when Bruce asked him for his drink order and the man spoke quickly in a heavy Scots accent, "Would ye have a whusky laddie?"

"Jeez where are you from mate?" said Bruce.

The man searched Bruce's face with a steely gaze, to see if he was being made fun of, and evidently realised that the barman was pure of heart. After a moment's hesitation he replied, "We are over on the ship from Scotland and this place by the sea is the first real look we have had at Australia, and it is a wee bit too hot for my liking, as I miss the cool mists of my native land."

"Golly thought Bruce, I won't ask him anything again." Bruce absorbed this news from the dour Scot and thought to himself that wintertime in Sydney can't be that hot but it is all relative as Scotland must be a cold old hole and pretty damn near as cold as good old Enngonia on a chilly winter's morning.

Bruce said, "Anyway here's your whisky, that will cool you down and what would you like for the little bloke?"

The man's face almost broke into a smile, "I would like an orange soda for the wee lad and then he can go off and play with the other children in back yard while I sip a few whuskies."

"Alright Mister one orange soda coming up," said Bruce as he topped up a glass with a Blue Bow Pelato orangeade for the little boy.

By this time sensing some entertainment some of the regulars had also gathered around and were examining the poor little fellow who looked back solemnly at them.

Just making conversation Bruce said, "Jeez mate what's that kid got on coz he looks a bit unhappy with it."

"He is wearing a kilt laddie, with our own tartan too, and he will get used to it. How about another Scotch Whusky there's a good fellow?" said the man and for the first time smiled fondly down at the wee manikin.

One of the wags who had sidled closer by now, by the name of O'Sullivan, an Irishman, said

"Well Jock it looks like his kilt is a teenie bit too long."

"Aye that it is, but he will grow into it," came the reply.

"Wots is name then?" asked one of the drinkers amiably.

"Wully, the same as mine but he is 'Wee Wully' and I am Wully."

"Cripes the poor lad," mumbled a wag from the back and turned away and smirked to his mate and whispered something which sent the man into stitches of laughter.

"Well you would be big Willie then?" Came the question from the comedian.

"Aye, that I am, he is wee and I'm not."

"How long are you staying here in Orstralia mate, are you here on holiday or something?" asked Bruce.

The Scot downed his scotch whisky and motioned for Bruce to give him another.

Wee Wullie looked a bit self-conscious with all the lads having a look

"Aye, we are here to play the bagpipes for the gathering and we can't wait to get back to Scotland and see some rain and green grass and perhaps you can pour me another Scotch whisky thash a good fellow," slurred the Scotsman who had, in the short time he was there, downed a few whiskies.

Time marched on and it was almost closing time so the Scotsman by now well and truly the worse for wear had downed his last whisky and headed for the door and was lost to sight.

Sometime later Bruce was just about ready to close up when a red faced lady came into the bar. She was panting lustily and stood there for a second with her head down and hands on her knees to suck in a few more lung-fulls of oxygen.

"Gidday, the Ladies Saloon bar is through there," said Bruce pointing with his chin as he polished a middy glass.

"Where is he? Where's mah 'Wee Wullie'?" gasped the lady, puffing mightily. "That damned fool husband of mine has just come home and I found he had left our wee lad behind."

Bruce thought for a while and it didn't take him long to work out that the lady who also talked with a Scots accent must have been connected with the visitor 'Big Willy' that afternoon. "Crikey lady, you must mean little Willy, coz if that's right, try out the back then coz he may still be there playing cricket with the other kids."

Not stopping for a thank you the lady flung herself away from the bar and stormed through the gathering throng of regulars in search of her precious Wee Wullie.

The mother and her young kilted son soon reappeared and without a word disappeared out of sight and the

78

bar returned to normal; while one of the jokers said "Wee Willy, well what do you know, what a name to give a fellow."

The regulars laughed and Bruce smiled as he moved down the bar to serve another beer.

Chapter 11

Milly the Maid Gets Help

Smiley the manager asked Bruce to wipe down the Pub Posters in their frames on the wall outside the Pub. Because of the dust, with the aid of the salt laden air from the onshore breeze, which had accumulated on the glass from the passing traffic.

Bruce marched outside armed with a large piece of old towel and a bucket of soapy water and set too with a will. Being a red blooded he-man Bruce was more interested in the posters depicting bathing suited beauties rather than the green clad Rugby Union players of the Randwick Team whose home was just up the road at the famous Club.

After a few minutes Bruce had finished his job and took all his gear back inside and cleaned up. Back at the bar pulling a beer, Bruce waited for the foam to settle into a nice collar. He shoved the foaming glass across the bar to the patron who tendered a pound note and waited for his change while Bruce rang up the sale.

Over the hubbub of the conversation in the bar and the grinding of the tram rolling past they could hear the Paper Boy yelling, "Papeeerrrz! Get yor paperrrzzz".

Bruce liked to read the paper and sneak a peek at the comics when Jane wasn't looking. He was always worried that she would think he hadn't grown up and of course that wasn't true. Just because he liked the funny cuts as his father called them did not make him a child. He always had a laugh at 'Bluey and Curley' about two larrikin mates. The comic strip made him sometimes think of the funny times at Booleroo sheep station where he worked before coming to the big smoke.

The small figure of Gazza the paper boy, with a fold of newspapers over one arm and a leather change purse over his shoulder, entered the bar and did a quick whip around the regulars to sell them the evening papers. Many of the drinkers were avid followers of the horses and would give everything a miss in the paper and immediately turn to the racing section in the last few pages at the back. The little chap sidled up to the bar and thrust a bank note onto the bar.

"Hello Gazzer would you like a pony of beer?" Enquired Bruce trying to be helpful.

Gazza looked up at Bruce and Jane who had just walked in, and snarled, through gritted teeth "Gimme anuder quid ah dinas!"

It took Bruce just a second to work out what Gazza had said but before he could jump too and accede to the little man's request, again Gazza snarled with a louder voice.

"Gimmee annuder quid ah dinnas!

"Er, here you are then as Bruce took the proffered pound note and gave the man a pounds worth of shilling pieces.

With no word of thanks Gazza snatched up the coins and thrust them into his change bag, wheeled about and stalked out of the bar.

A red faced Bruce looked up and turned to his sweetheart Jane, "Crikey what's got into him, he was an angry little bloke that's for sure?"

Jane smiled and said, "Well you did upset him by saying do you want a pony of beer".

"Well what's wrong with that?" said Bruce going a shade of red as he wracked his brains to see how he could have offended the Paper Boy who by this time had swung through the doors and disappeared.

"Well first of all you said a pony which is a five ounce glass usually reserved for ladies as most men drink a middy or a schooner. It is only a little glass of beer and he thought you were making a reference to him being small".

"Yeh, well it's true he is a very small bloke!"

"Yes he is but you don't have to remind him. You see Gazza was a jockey who was warned off the course for aggressive riding, and when you asked about a pony of beer he thought you had been laughing at him, not only because he was small but because he was heaved out of the saddle so as to speak. Well that is what I imagine was eating him anyway."

"Crikey, I would never had thought of that. It's complicated and these city slickers are a real touchy mob, it was easier to talk with Bluey than this lot, and he was next to useless. I've had enough for one day, nothing else can go wrong can it?"

No sooner had the words escaped Bruce's mouth that he felt a tug on his arm and looked around to see Milly the Maid looking up at him. Her round grandmotherly face, framed by white hair pulled back in a bun, was wreathed in a look of concern.

"Oh, come quickly Bruce can you come and help. The cook has got into the cooking sherry again and is throwing the pots and pans and anything else in reach around the kitchen," Milly wailed as she again pulled at Bruce's arm to get him to follow her.

"Jeez Milly where is Smiley, can't he fix her? He is never around when you want him, It's not fair I always get caught with the problems around here, after all he is the manager," grumbled Bruce.

Jane who was standing close by listening to this exchange gave her usual good natured chuckle and said, "Bruce don't be so mean go and help Milly. I am sure you will sort it all out."

Bruce noticed that Jane started to drift away back towards the hall and it looked like he was going to be stuck with old Milly and the sozzled cook.

"Alright Milly old girl lead me to her, I'll be right behind you. A fat lot of good you are Jane," called Bruce to Jane's retreating back.

Jane waived her hand in the air and very smartly disappeared back into her office with a derisory chuckle echoing in his ears.

Turning to the barman on duty Bruce called out, "Alright Bill you hold the fort and serve the regulars while I will go and help Milly sort out cook."

"Take your time Brucie, glad it's you and not me fixing up cook she is a terror when she has a few glasses of cooking sherry aboard."

Bruce followed Milly the maid and the closer he got to the kitchen the louder the racket became. There was loud singing from cook and banging of things as if they were being thrown against the walls. He entered the kitchen and the little lady who did the cooking stood there swaying with one hand around the neck of a Penfolds Sweet Sherry bottle, while with the other hand she hurled a pot which bounced off the wall that then came to rest on the tiled floor with a clatter.

"Crikey Milly, I don't like the look in her eye, I saw a horse once like that up at Booleroo Sheep Station and the flaming thing bit me!" whispered Bruce out the side of his mouth to the hapless maid as they both stood there staring at the cook who was swaying alarmingly.

Bruce gave it his best shot and tried the diplomatic way, "Now what are you up to cookie, I reckon it is a good idea if you get yourself off home and come in when you're feeling better, what do you reckon?"

"Arr, go and bang your head, yah silly looking thing" came the slurred reply accompanied with a cackle and another pot whizzed overhead and Milly and Bruce ducked.

Bruce decided to be more forceful with his next try, "Now come on cookie there's a nice lady, how about you leave the pots and pans for us to clean up and you get on home and put your feet up."

"Yeh, and you go and put your head in a bucket, stupid," came the reply from the drunken cook who stood there swaying as she blew a stray lock of hair off her face with a "Pfffwheet." And a frypan banged against the stove and joined its brethren on the floor.

"Right Milly, I've got a brilliant plan, you wait here and I will go and get Smiley he can't have gone too far. Hooroo" and with that Bruce beat a hasty retreat and went searching for reinforcements as the wails from Milly of "Don't leave me!" faded in the distance. A last raspberry blown by the cook could also be heard as he fled.

He could only guess what they eventually did with the old gal. Most probably tied her up with barbed wire and sheared her or something. Hopefully Smiley had sorted it all out.

The cook stood there swaying with a bottle of cooking sherry in one hand

Luckily he and his beloved Jane had time off from work that afternoon and it was a good excuse to escape early that day from the hotel and the frightening time spent in the kitchen with the crazy cook. Milly would not have him on her good fellow list either after abandoning her as he did.

When he met up with Jane she immediately mentioned the kitchen incident, "Before we do anything Bruce I heard that you had and interesting morning with cookie and Milly is still getting over it."

"Yup, that cook is a terror alright Janie, when she has had a few glasses of that cooking sherry."

"Hm, Bruce I heard you had fled and left poor Milly to sort it out. Anyhow how about we go for a drive Bruce? Dad has an old car we can use and you can have a go at driving too."

"I couldn't help it Janie not that I am a coward or anything like that, I just thought that Cookie mighta ripped me up a bit or something. Anyhow Jane the drive sounds beaut; what sort of car is it, I reckon I should get me licence coz I did a bit up the bush in the truck?"

"Dad has had the Ford Pilot for years now and it is sort of his hobby car although it is a bit old now."

They collected the car and in no time the two young lovers were ready to get moving. Greta the Alsatian dog came along also and sat in the back, and hung her head out of the window to chew at the wind that flew past.

They drove to the Gap at Watsons Bay and then drove down the steep and winding road to Rose Bay, where the old Second World War sea planes were dragged up on the shore.

Jane brought the car to a stop in the large car park and suggested that Bruce try his hand at driving. They swapped seats and Bruce had a good look at the controls.

"This looks simple enough Janie, pretty much the same as the truck back in the bush so hang on and we can drive a bit here."

The car did a few kangaroo hops as Bruce was getting used to the clutch and Greta in the back seat got the message loud and clear and she pulled her head back out of the window and lay down on the back seat and hid her head under her paws.

Greta was a nervous back seat driver and hid her head in her paws

"I think that you could do with a bit more practice Bruce because Greta is lying down and looking a bit uncomfortable".

Bruce laughed as the car did a few more hops and shuddered to a halt and the engine stopped.

"Crickey, the flaming thing has run outta petrol what rotten luck," moaned Bruce.

"Just a suggestion Bruce, when you wish to stop just put your foot on the clutch and put the car out of gear, because if you don't then it stalls the engine. How about you slide over and I will get it started again. I think that is enough driving for you today."

Bruce smiled and shrugged, "Jeez, it doesn't look that hard but I will get the knack of it sooner or later. Anyhow Greta is looking happier already, coz she has her head stuck outta the back window already."

Chapter 12

The Boys from Booleroo

"**B**rucie are you there?" Came the faint voice out of the hand held earpiece of the old wall phone.

"Yes, Bruce is here and I will get 'im for you just hang on a mo," replied Smiley.

"Bruce there's a call for ya and it's a long distance one," yelled the bar manager as he dropped the phone and let it swing in the breeze as he sauntered off.

Bruce stopped cleaning the beer glasses and meandered out of the bar to the hall to take the call.

"Gidday, this is Bruce, whose there?"

"Hello mate this is Whippy, your old pal from Booleroo, can ya hear me?" Came the voice as if it was coming from the other side of the moon.

"Gidday Whippy old mate, good to hear from ya, but you will have to yell coz the party line is a bit wonky."

"OK, the fellows are coming down on the train for a couple of days and all of 'em are looking forward to seeing yah. Are there any rooms at the hotel for us to stay?"

"Of course there are mate, how many of the boys will be coming?"

"Well there will be Skeeter, Blackie, Jackie and meself of course".

"You mean Jackie is coming too, I can't believe it he must be back from walkabout then but he has never been to a big town before, let alone seen the ocean. I reckon he will be in for a big shock."

Whippy laughed and said, "Yeh, it will be interesting when we see the look on his face when he has a gander at the big billabong, he will go pale with shock."

"Well when you come we will have a couple of rooms for you and you can share with whoever you like except it nots gonna be Jane, ha ha." laughed Bruce.

Over the next few days Bruce was always telling Jane about his mates on Booleroo Sheep Station, out in the donga near Enngonia. Jane was a very patient young woman, but eventually even the name of Booleroo set her teeth on edge. She would say how much she was looking forward to meeting Bruce's friends. Anything to stop the ceaselessly, 'Whippy did this, or Skeeter said that, or Jackie went walkabout again.

Early for work on the Saturday Bruce was surprised to see a large group of men in the main bar with the regulars gathered around them.

At the centre of the group was a portly fellow with a bald head and his coat was fastened with one button and stretched across his midriff as if the coat was a few sizes too small. Judging by the size of him that fellow is a tooth merchant thought Bruce. He watched the man strut around self-importantly as a few of the crowd clustered around him wrote busily in note pads.

On taking up his accustomed place behind the bar, Bruce asked Bill the barman, "Crikey Billie, who is the porky geezer over there in the too tight coat?"

"Yeh he is a bigun that's for sure, yonder is our local member, Walter Brownstone MP, the famous politician,

90

a Member of Parliament, and he has lobbed in here to be interviewed by the newspaper reporters about his opinion on the evils of alcohol."

Bruce straightened up at that announcement and looked over at the portly figure of Mr. Brownstone and he immediately took a dislike to the man. The MP was pointing his finger at the bottles behind the bar and in a loud voice was telling his audience, "As I've been saying chaps I am absolutely against the use of alcohol and its effects on our fellow man. Look about you at these poor misguided souls and you will see before you the men who habitually become drunk and disorderly, these the poor souls who frequent this establishment."

The regulars looked at each other and some smirked, some laughed and others gave a few rude gestures. The man's voice droned on and despite the wise cracks and rude comments from the regulars he never stopped for breath.

Bruce called out to the crowd who had invaded the quiet confines of the Auckland Hotel, "Gentlemen it's a hot day perhaps you would like to lean on the bar and Bill and I will get you some cool drinks to whet your whistles."

Suddenly the MP was abandoned as all the crowd left him standing there. In no time there was a pushing and shouting mob of reporters, hanger ons and regulars at the bar yelling out their orders for beer, whisky and stout.

The politician gathered himself and knowing that he had temporarily lost his audience resolved to make the best of a bad deal. He too pushed his way through the throng and eyeballed Bruce and with a self-important voice bellowed to be heard above the noise, "Now see here young man I want a lemon squash and make sure it has plenty of ice in it."

"Of course Mr. Brownstone, coming right up as soon as I can pour it for you," called Bruce as he winked at Bill the barman who catching on, smirked and hid his smile with his hand.

Bruce grabbed a schooner glass and put ice in it, then three servings of Gin and then filled up the glass with Blue Bow Lemon Squash.

"Here you are Mister," said Bruce as he slid the large glass filled to the brim over to the local Poli.

The thirsty politician intent on ridding the world of all drinkers of the demon drink grabbed the glass with no thanks to Bruce and downed it in one long swallow. Apart from going red and giving a small cough or two the man announced, "That hit the spot alright and indeed I am very thirsty doing all that talking to the representatives of the Nation's finest newspapers. It has given me a desire to have another lemon squash, there's a good fellow."

Bruce happy to oblige set too with a will and this time poured in four measures of Gin and slid the glass over to the MP who for some reason or other missed at his first attempt, but closed one eye and eventually grabbed the drink. Now Mr. Brownstone was no fool. He knew a good glass of lemon squash when he had one and these drinks at the good old Auckland Hotel were the best he had ever had.

After a few hours many of the politician's audience had drifted away and the reporters had wobbled out of the hotel to return to their desks with eloquent stories fuelled by the free drinks from the generous MP. The bar was still noisy however, as Mr. Brownstone was singing a sad song to a blowsy looking drinker asleep at one of the tables.

"Jusht call me Wally young fella," slurred the red faced politician as he ordered another round of drinks for the bar from Bruce.

Bruce looked around the main bar of the hotel and smiled, "I reckon Mr. Walter Brownstone MP, may change his policy on alcohol what do you think Bill?"

A few days later, on Wednesday morning, when Bruce went to open the hotel's front doors he was momentarily surprised to see a group of men who looked vaguely familiar, all waiting patiently to gain entry. It took but a split second to see that it was some of his old mates from Booleroo, who all yelled "Gidday Brucie, give us a beer!"

"Jeez it's good to see youse all. Come on in and meet Jane she has heard a lot about yah."

All the fellows trooped in all talking at once. Jane came out of the office to see what all the noise was about and was greeted by shouts from all the yobboes, "Gidday Jane, what a corker Brucie, gidday Jane, and owaryerz," and so on.

Jane smiled broadly and gave them all a welcome and looked at the scruffy lot who had just come down from the bush, they all looked like they had slept sitting up on a train. Which they had.

The bleary eyed country boys were an interesting spectacle. Whippy still had his broad brimmed hat perched on the back of his head and Skeeter, the diminutive drover, had on a green football jersey which barely fitted him as he must have snitched it from someone's clothes line.

What a scruffy mob but Bruce was glad his mates had come to visit him at Bondi.

"Boys, I will phone Bluey over at the fish shop and he can come on over and catch up on all the news," yelled Bruce above the noise from the drovers who were all talking at once to the lovely Jane. Anyone would think they hadn't seen a pretty girl for a while, and they would be absolutely correct as there is not much up on Booleroo sheep station in the way of females except for a few thousand ewes.

"Crikey, Brucie do yah have to, Bluey may get lost on the way," was a comment from one of the boys which they all found very funny.

"Get your gear into your rooms boys and then you can have a good look around the hotel and the Bondi beach sights. Meet back here out front in 10 minutes and we can get started," said Jane who was enjoying the attention.

In no time the gang from Booleroo were waiting out the front of the hotel studying the framed beer posters when Bruce, Jane and Greta her faithful dog, came out to meet them.

"Alright everybody, let's go on down to the beach so Jackie can have a look at the ocean and when he has had enough we can wander along the walkway around the beach, have an ice-cream and get back to the pub for a beer. Everybody in favour of that?"

A chorus of "too rights" greeted the announcement from Jane.

The drovers from the bush seemed to be looking forward to the walk around the beach and no doubt the bathing beauties were more of an interest than looking at sand and water. Jackie on the other hand showed little signs of emotion on his dark face and was his usual stolid self.

In no time they came closer to the beach and all were watching Jackie's first reaction when he had his first look at the Tasman Sea. It was one of those glorious days that Bondi is famous for all over the world. Blue sky overhead with no clouds, an ocean that was smooth and a deep blue out further past the breakers. The water close in was a green gradually appearing as clear as liquid glass closer in to shore. The waves were not large but just rolled in and hardly broke against the shore.

Jackie by this time could hear the sound of the beach, the waves mounting the shore and the shouts of the children laughing and gambolling in their games. Looking up he saw the scores of seagulls wheeling overhead and he quickened his pace to see what awaited him.

He had never seen water in such abundance. The most water he had seen was in the Darling River near Bourke and also a billabong of water that had grown into a lagoon one wet season. The countryside where Jackie and his tribe came from was in the far West of New South Wales up near the Queensland border and it was flat, scrub covered and dusty and that was in the wet season. (Just joking). The wet season did come but it just made the ground muddy in places and the grasses grew greener. Nowhere would there be a large amount of water to compare to the beachside of Bondi.

He quickly ran down to the water and waded in and stood there looking out to sea and with his arms spread wide. Everyone followed him down to the water's edge and watched what the aboriginal boy would do.

Turning from looking at the ocean, Whippy spoke quietly, "Look Bruce these aboriginals are very spiritual people, note how he has raised his arms to the Great Spirit."

Bruce noticed Jackie standing there with his arms outstretched and couldn't resist asking him and raising his voice to be heard over the sound of the waves said, "Hey, Jackie we see you are honouring the Great Spirit and raising your arms in praise."

"Nah Bruce I'm just trying to stop 'em getting wet," came the answer from Enngonia's finest and everyone had a laugh at that one.

Despite the efforts to remain dry, Jackie managed to get his trousers wet and trembling with excitement he turned to all his friends with a beaming smile, "Boys that was plurry good I not seen such a large Billabong before and what's on the other side?"

"There is a country called New Zealand over there," said Bruce.

Bruce was content here he was at Bondi with his two mates.

"Never heard of that place what tribe belongs there?" asked Jackie with a surprised look on his face.

"The people are called Maoris and they are a big tribe in more ways than one. The men are well built with slabs of muscle and the women are not much different," said Bruce with a laugh and everyone joined in.

Jackie thought for a while and Bruce could see the man's mind working away with this latest news. Eventually Jackie's face cleared of its frown and a big smile wreathed his face. "Maori tribe would not stay big if they lived up at Enngonia, they would all be skinny like my tribe. Eating kangaroo and goanna tastes bad."

With that statement and the solution to the Maoris weight problems solved Jane suggested they go down to the beach front for a look at the surf while the boys from the bush have a few beers and soak up the atmosphere of the Auckland Hotel.

A little later sitting on the wall overlooking the famous beach Bruce looked at Jane and Jane looked at Bruce, "Jeez Janie I hope the cook is off the sweet sherry otherwise baked beans on toast would be the only baked dinner the boys from Booleroo will have tonight."

"Yes, and perhaps Greta would like a nice sausage to munch on too. What do you think my darling little doggie?"

"Woof," came the reply from the eating machine on four legs.

Chapter 13

Mr. Poleford checks out

The boys from Booleroo Sheep Station had paid a visit to Bruce and so far had enjoyed their trip. The most popular part being the young ladies sunbathing on the famous beach. The fellows were starved for female company where they worked on the sheep station and were excited to see so many beautiful girls lying around getting toasted on all sides. All agreed that when Bruce worked as a Jackeroo with them he had driven everyone mad reminiscing about Bondi Beach but now they could well and truly understand why he missed it so much.

Back then Bruce was always whingeing about how hot and dry it was on Booleroo and the flies drove him crazy. He would often talk about the surf, the sheilas and the ice creams; and so many times that everyone knew his litany of woe off by heart.

After spending some time down at the beach and giving Jackie the black tracker a look at the water, the group of happy young people and one large Alsatian dog returned to the Auckland Hotel. They poured into the main bar laughing and talking loudly and were looking forward to a cool drink or two.

Scarcely had they settled down and the barman had taken their orders for beers all round; there was a commotion, and Milly the maid, the hotel's housekeeper, came quickly into the public bar. She hesitated for a second and when she saw Bruce made her way straight to him waving her arms in the air. Bruce saw the pale faced matron bearing down on him and knew with a sinking heart that she was the bearer of bad news.

Halting in front of Bruce, the stout lady in the white apron said in an agitated voice "Brucie we have a problem, I think Mr. Poleford in room eight has died. I can't get him to wake up. Will you come with me and see fer yerself?"

"Crikey, why does it always have to be me?" Grizzled Bruce.

Bruce looked at Jane and quickly told her what the problem was. The group of drovers overheard his muttered announcement and as one they all volunteered to go with Bruce to give him a hand.

"Jeez, Milly can't Smiley go and fix it, I don't wanna be around a dead person?"

"I think he is in town today Bruce, it's his day orf and you have gotta help. Just don't stand there come and help!" grumbled Milly as she pulled at Bruce's arm.

"Well let's wait until he gets back then."

"Bruce!" said Jane and fixed him with the skinny eyed look that he was beginning to be familiar with.

Bruce got the message and he and Jane with the group of drovers following the broad behind of Milly who soon arrived at the door to room number eight. Milly used her house key to gain entry to the room where sure enough the form of the late Mr. Poleford was lying motionless on the bed. A glass and bottle of Bond 7 Whisky was empty on the bedside table beside him.

The room smelled of stale whisky and a few flies were lazily doing wheelies over the face of the corpse.

Bruce smirked, "Well look at that, it didn't take long for the flies to get here from Booleroo."

"This is not the time to joke Bruce this is serious, what are we going to do?" said Jane with a frown.

"Looks like he had too much to drink and killed hiself," said Skeeter to his mate Whippy, who agreed with a nod of his head.

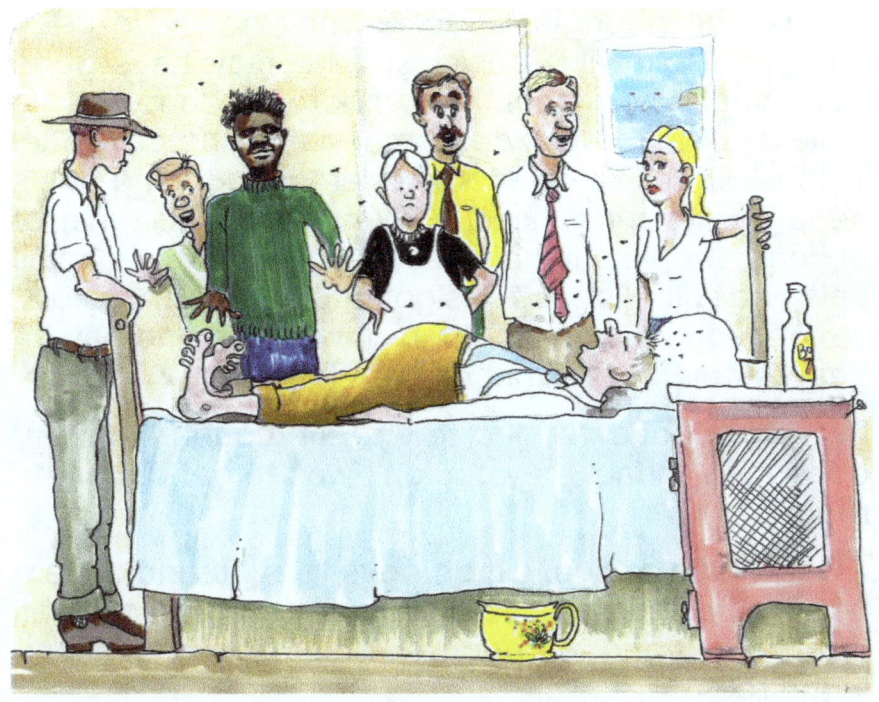

They all stood there silently while the flies buzzed over Mr. Poleford's still form.

The group of friends now quiet and serious all gathered around the body of Mr. Poleford. Whippy suggested that they have a try at resuscitating him. Skeeter poked and prodded the body to see if there was any life in it. Blackie grabbed the body by the shoulders and gave it a good shake and Mr. Poleford's head rolled this way and that until Jane put a hand on Blackie's arm and shook her head to get him to stop.

"Jeez he's dead alright, I reckon we should call the police," said Skeeter with a tremor in his voice.

"Nah, git 'im a Doctor or an ambilance, poor man," said Milly who was standing there looking on with a worried look on her face, as Jane hurriedly left the room to make the emergency telephone call.

Jackie, the aboriginal tracker, may not have been too good following tracks and he may have gone walkabout when there was work to be done, but he believed he knew a dead man when he saw one. With a serious voice and a vehement nodding of his head, Jackie announced, "Crikey, boys I've seen a lot of dead people and he's dead alright, jist lookit 'im all pale and still. His spirit has gone to join his ancestors, so I reckon we should all go downstairs and have a beer to celebrate. What do you think?"

Everyone looked at Jackie and all thought it a very good idea, in fact they couldn't wait to get out of the room.

"Good idea Jackie, c'mon boys let's go and have a beer," said the quietly spoken Whippy and they all trooped out and left poor Mr. Poleford's body alone in the room.

In no time the boys from Booleroo had jostled their way down the stairs in a race to be the first at the bar. After a while when they were starting on their second beer the conversation soon moved away from the late Mr. Poleford's sad departure and turned to more important subjects. Topics such as what was the best beer Tooheys or Reschs and whether Australia's first eleven cricket team would bring home the Ashes or was the blonde sheila in the red bathing suit down at the beach a film star coz she looked a corker.

Suddenly, Jackie gave a low cry and pointed with a quivering finger down to the end of the bar, his face was pale, well paler than usual, and perspiration shone on his face, "Look boys Mr. Poleford's spirit has returned!"

All conversation stopped and as one all the drinkers turned to where Jackie was pointing. A gasp of fear was heard from all as there standing before them was the late Mr. Poleford at the end of the bar.

"Jackie, I thought you said he was dead and you had a lot of experience with dead people?" said Bruce.

Jackie was still in shock staring at the apparition standing there. Before he could reply the dead man wiped his forehead with the back of his hand and spoke to the barman with a weak voice. "Can I have another whisky there's a good fellow, in fact make it a double."

"Now that doesn't sound like a dead man to me, it would seem that too much whisky knocked the old coot out and Blackie shaking him must have done the trick. Well done Blackie," Jane said with a smile.

"Jeez fellas, seeing Mr. Poleford arisen from the dead gave me a real fright. Let's make sure that Jackie is OK now, coz he looks like Mr. Poleford did half an hour ago."

They all stood there shaken as they stared at the dishevelled figure of Mr. Poleford. Jackie was especially frightened and was shaking from head to toe. Bruce was patting him on the back looking concerned at the shaking warrior from Enngonia's finest.

"I shouldn't have come to the Big Smoke and shoulda stayed back on my tribal land," moaned Jackie all pale and sweating.

"There, there Jackie never mind, now come and have another beer mate," said Skeeter.

A little later Jane and Bruce drew closer and smiled into each other's eyes. Raising his glass he murmured, "Well Jane I could not be happier, you know. My mates here from Booleroo, you by my side and Mr. Poleford possibly arisen from the dead."

Jane looked over Bruce's shoulder and saw the unsteady figure making its way towards them, "I am happy to hear it Bruce but watch out here comes Mr. Poleford, he looks like he has something on his mind."

"I say Bruce old chap, hic, I seem to have lost my room," ……. mumbled the ghostly apparition recently arisen from the dead.

"Yeh you had better phone the ambulance Janie and tell 'em not to bother to come. However, he may need a doctor tomorrow morning coz Mr. Poleford looks like he is going to have a giant hangover."

"Now Mr. Poleford I will get Milly to help you back to your room, would you like to do that?" asked Jane with a frown of concern on her beautiful face.

"Yesh thash would be shplendid," slurred the now apparently alive guest from room number eight.

Later that day Bruce was walking down the hall and met Jane as she was coming out of the office.

"By the way Bruce what is happening with your friends from the country, will we be showing them any more of the sights while they are down here in Sydney?" asked Jane.

"Well Jane sorry, it's too late coz they are not here anymore, they've gorn off home."

"They've gone home! What on earth for, I thought they were down here to see Sydney and have a good time catching up with you on all the news."

"Well, all the boys voted to get back on the train and shoot through back to the bush as there were too many cars, too many buildings and far too many people for their liking down here."

"I suppose the resurrection of Mr. Poleford didn't help much either, said Jane with a laugh.

"Yeh, especially Mr. Polfeord," said Bruce with a smile.

"It's funny though isn't it? I enjoy working in the hotel Jane and I wouldn't dream of going with the boys back to the bush. Although I was talking with a bloke at the Real Estate Agents the other day when I was walking to work and his job sounds real interesting and pays well. I may have a gander at that, what do you reckon?"

"Oh, Bruce."

THE END

Glossary

English is a language of many accents and can be virtually unintelligible between someone living in Brisbane in Australia to someone living in Manchester in England.

To make matters worse many Australians talk through their nose. They also run all their words together. For example Didjahaveagoodweekend? This means did you have a good week end away from work.

This manner of speaking most probably has something to do with the flies. Australia is a country full of sheep you see. Just try holding your nose and start speaking and that is how to do it and make sure you keep your mouth, almost closed to keep the flies out and lo' you are speaking Strine. Strine being the Australian patois of English. If this doesn't work then at least stop your top lip from moving.

Compared to the deeper tones of many Americans, for example John Wayne and Garry Cooper they did not talk through their noses. One can only assume that sitting for hours in a wagon rolling across the prairie must have given them deeper voices.

Now the English talk with their eye brows raised and their heads held high with their nose in the air. That is how to speak their form of English. Just try it sometime.

The New Zealanders however, talk like all the above. They speak through their nose, raise their eye brows and most probably travel everywhere in wagons. To speak Kiwi just do all of the above and substitute every letter E with I, I with U and you can now speak like a native of New Zealand. Easy isn't it?

Now the language in some parts of Australia is called Strine. Bruce and some of his mates speak Strine that is really a form of English with some shortening of words, inclusion of colloquial sayings and remember, managing to avoid swallowing too many flies.

I hope that you could understand and enjoy this book and urge you to read Bruce's first book called "Adventures of a Jackeroo. It will be easier for you, because by now you can read and understand Strine. There have been many comments from readers who have found the Glossary of use, therefore I have made sure that we have included this helpful aid in this second book in the Bruce from Bondi series of adventures.

+++++++++++++++++++

A

Alsatian Dog – now called a German shepherd

All Blacks – the famous New Zealand Rugby Union football team

Ambilance - ambulance

Annuder – another

Ashes – the cricket trophy for the winner of the cricket series between England and Australia

Auckland Hotel Bondi – named after the largest city in New Zealand, Auckland on the North Island.

B

Bagpipes – the best musical instrument in the world, or so the Scots say.

Banjo Patterson – a favourite bush poet in Australia

Bar fly – a person who is a habitual attender of the hotel bar

Bard – a poet

Beaut Sheila – beautiful, a good looking or a nice girl

Beg – New Zealand for big. They have a habit of substituting I for E

Beudy- beauty, beautiful

Big Smoke – a countryman's term for the city

Bigun – she was a big one, a bigun.

Billabong – a lagoon, waterhole, a small body of water

Blimey – an exclamation like 'Golly' etc

Bloke – Australian for boy, man, mate etc

Blue Bow – a manufacturer of soft drinks, sodas

Bondi Beach – a popular surfing beach and tourist destination close to Sydney the main city in the state of New South Wales. It is also popular with the New-Zealanders who arrive in Australia.

Bloody – an exclamation or a word to use in Australia to describe something. For example she is bloody good looking, it was bloody bad luck etc.

Bloke – man, friend, mate

Bludger – someone who is lazy or doesn't like hard work

Bluey – a nick name in Australia for anyone who is ginger or red headed,

Bluey and Curley – a very popular comic strip of the time about two friends in the Australian bush.

Bond 7 Whisky – an Australian brand of whisky, very good medicine.

108

Brekkie – breakfast

Bro – Brother, New Zealand for mate.

Brucie – a form of affection for someone called Bruce

Brudder – Aboriginal term for brother

Bunging – assuming, putting on - bunging on an act

C

Cardboard suitcase – a valise, port made of hardened varnished cardboard.

Chips – Australian term for French fries

Chipper – feeling good or looking well

Chop – not much chop, means not too good

Chups – New Zealand for chips (French fries) they also substitute I for U, don't ask why, they just do

Chalk up - write up

Choc top – an ice-cream in a cone and the ice cream topped with chocolate.

City Slickers – someone who lives in the big smoke, a city resident

Clobber – English/cockney term for clothes

Cobber – pal, mate, a friend

Coldie – slang for a cold beer, a beer

Coot – an old coot, an old man

Corker – a good sort, a good looking girl, car, horse etc

Coulda – could have, like coulda, shoulda (should have), woulda (would have)

Coz – a shortening of because

Crikey – an exclamation like Golly etc

D

Daily Mirror - an evening newspaper in Sydney

Daft Bugger – a silly fellow

Didja – did you?

Dinas – pronounced Deenahs – a dina is a shilling in the old currency now equivalent to a ten cent piece

Ditch – abandon, get rid of

Dogs – Greyhound racing, dog races

Dolled up – prettied up, an attempt to look good

Donga – Way out in the countryside, the bush.

Donged – hit, pronounced 'dong..ed'

Drippy - silly

Drover – a sheep, cattle herder,

E

Elastic sided boots – riding and work boots with no laces but elastic sided to firmly stay on the foot

'Er – her

Eucalyptus – a gum tree, native to Australia, there are hundreds of different types. Dogs love them.

F

Fantails – a chocolate covered caramel toffy, candy

Feet – a third of a metre

Fellas – fellows

Fedora – a felt wide brimmed hat with an indented crown.

Fer - for

First Eleven – the cricket team which represents Australia

Flag Ale — a popular beer produced by Tooheys the makers of the best beer in the world.

Flamin' — flaming a descriptive word an exclamation like Golly, Bloody etc

Flat out like a lizard drinking — very busy

Flipper — an arm

Footie — football, covering the three codes of Rugby Union, Rugby League and Australian Rules

Footie matches — games of football

Footpath - sidewalk

Forward — a large and strong player of football in the forward part of the pack or team

Full bottle — meaning one hundred percent or alright

Full quid — alright, OK, also can mean someone is sane or in command of his senses.

Funny cuts - comics

G

Galahs — a pink, white and grey parrot of the drier parts of the country. They are not known for their intellect.

Gander — a good look at something

G and T — a cool alcoholic drink made of Gin, tonic and ice with a slice of lemon.

Gap — The Gap - the opening to Sydney Harbour near Watson's Bay between two cliffs

Gazzer or Gazza — a friendly form of Garry, example Bazza (Barry), Wazza (Warwick)

Geezer — and old bloke or man.

Get cracking — to get moving faster

Getoutavit – get out of it

Gev – New Zealand for give

Gidday – good day, hello

Gimme – give me

Gimme anudder quid o' dinnas – give me another quid (pound note now $2) of shillings (now ten cents)

Git – New Zealand for 'get',

Git orf - get off me

Giveusah – give us a, beer, hit in the head or a kiss. Give me etc.

Goanna – a large lizard can grow to six feet or 2 metres in length.

Goin' - going

Golly – an exclamation

Gorn – gone

Gunna – going to, a gunna can also mean a lazy person, meaning he is always going to do something but never gets around to it.

H

Haka - (plural is the same as singular: *haka*) is a traditional ancestral war cry, dance, or challenge from the Māori people of New Zealand. Thrilling to watch.

Hang of it – getting to know how to do something – to understand

Hang on a mo – wait a moment or wait a minute.

Havetuh – have to

Hellavah – hell of a

Hev – New Zealand for have

Heinz – the maker of the best baked beans in the world. They made Australians what they are today

Hiself – himself

Hold the fort – stay and look after things

Hood – the bonnet or engine covering of a car

Hubbub – noise

I

'im – him

Ice Berg – **Ice Bergers** – a group of older men who swim all year around at Bondi beach rock pool, even in winter when the water can be rather cold.

J

Jock – a nick name for someone from Scotland

Jake – all right, example - she will be all right

Jackeroo – a trainee manager of a sheep station or cattle station, farm. Jillaroo is the female.

Jaffas – an orange coloured candy coated chocolate ball, about the size of a moth ball.

Jeez – an exclamation

Jist - just

Jumbo – someone who is big, something big

K

Kangaroo – a marsupial with a large tail and which hops by using its large two back legs

Kia Ora – New Zealand Maori language for a greeting – be well, be healthy or hello

Kilt – a Highland Scots tartan skirt. Usually worn by the men from Scotland.

Kinda – kind of

Kiwi – a New Zealander named after the unique native flightless bird with the very long curved beak.

Kuck – New Zealand for, kick

L

Ladies Lounge – see Ladies Saloon bar

Ladies Saloon Bar, Salon – in the 1950's the ladies had to drink in a separate part of the hotel. They were not permitted to drink in the public bar with the lads.

Land of the Long White Cloud – the country of New Zealand

Laughing gear - teeth

Learning the ropes – most probably sailors used this term which means learning how to do things

Lino – a covering for the floor, see linoleum

Linoleum – (informally abbreviated to lino) An early form of floor covering made from materials such as solidified linseed oil (linoxyn), pine rosin, ground cork dust, wood flour, covering for the floor

Lobbed in – Just arrived

Lobbed a ball – thrown a ball (confusing isn't it?)

M

Mailman – the postman, the Postie

Maurie – an affectionate name for someone called Maurice

Mate – a pal, a buddy, everyone is usually called mate in Australia

Maori – the native Polynesian of New Zealand – a great people and much loved.

Mah – my (Scots)

Middy – a 10 fluid ounce glass of beer

Mighta — might of

Milko — the man who delivers the milk to the houses and businesses by horse and cart.

Mirror — The Daily Mirror, a newspaper popular at the time

Mo — moment, minute. Hold on a mo.

Mob — a herd of sheep, a group of people

Moleskin trousers — made from Moleskin which is a heavy cotton fabric, woven and then sheared to create a short, soft pile on one side.

N

New South Wales — one of the States in Australia

New Zealand — a country south of Australia, where they speak a different accent form of English. The land is inhabited by people called Kiwis. Many Kiwis come to live in Australia and make Bondi their home. Sensible people the Kiwis.

Nuffink — Australian, a sometime pronunciation of the word "Nothing"

O

Okey Dokey – alright, OK

Old Dart — the Australians sometime refer to England as back home, or the Old Dart.

Old Bag — an old lady, old woman

Old currency — pre-decimal currency (before 1966) when Australia had pounds, shillings and pence

Onyer — on you, like goodonyer – good on you.

OP Rum — Overproof red rum made by the best rum maker in the world Bundaberg. It cures most ills and can be used as sheep dip, aeroplane fuel, light fires, put out fires, acne ointment and paint stripper.

Orf – off, git orf (get off)

Orstralia – Strine way of saying Australia

Owareyerz – How are you? Some Australians can regrettably run their words together and speak through their nose. We can understand Americans though, because we have a lot of TV shows from the USA. However they can't understand us. Thank God for subtitles. We on the other hand have difficulty in understanding some provincial accents from the United Kingdom.

P

Paper Boy – someone who sells the daily newspapers. They are not always boys but we still call them Paper Boys - Have you ever heard of a paper man?

Pain in the butt – a problem

Paperz – the very clever cry that the paper boy calls when he is selling newspapers. After all what else would he cry out?

Penny – old currency equivalent to a cent

Pennies - see Penny, plural for penny

Personality – Bruce's theme song, Personality sung by the American popular singer, Lloyd Price.

Pims – a drink for the ladies. Pimm's No. 1 Cup is based on gin and can be served either on ice or in cocktails. It has a dark-tea colour with a reddish tint, and tastes subtly of spice and citrus fruit. Said to cure all ills such as baldness and bad breath. Have you ever seen a bald lady?

Pint – a very large glass of beer 20 Fluid ounces

Plurry – aboriginal dialect of the white man's 'Bloody'. It was plurry good etc

Poli – a politician, sometimes a figure of fun or satire in Australia

Pommie – someone who comes from England, Australians love them.

Pommie git – an Englishman who has been short changed in the IQ stakes.

Ponged – smells, something on the nose.

Pony of Beer – a 5 fluid ounce glass, very small drink. Ladies drink from Ponies.

Poor sod – poor fellow, used when you are sorry for someone.

Porky – someone who is over-weight as opposed to skinny

Port – Fortified wine, sweet with some brandy added

Postie – the mailman or postman

Pound – the old currency – a pound note equivalent to $2

Pub – a hotel – derived from the Public House, English.

Put a cork in it – keep quiet

Q

Queensland – one of the States in Australia

Quid – Australian for a pound note (pre decimal currency) equivalent to $2

R

Randwick Rugby Union Club – Randwick is a suburb close to Bondi. It is the home of a very successful Rugby Union football club. The home of the magnificent footballer Ken Catchpole. Why mention Mr. Catchpole? Well I just like seeing his name.

Real Estate Agent – a Realtor, one who sells real estate

Regular – a drinker at the hotel

Reschs – Reschs Pilsener – a popular brand of beer

Rollers – waves rolling in to surf on

Rugby – Rugby Union a code of football popular in some parts of Australia

S

Sallies – an affectionate name for the Salvation Army

Salvoes – also and affectionate name for the Salvation Army

Schooner – a 15 fluid ounce glass of beer

Sec – hang on a sec, second (as in stop for a moment)

Scone – pronounced 'skon', head. You know something that sits on your shoulders.

Set to – to begin

Shandy – a drink for the ladies, made from 50% beer and 50% lemonade

Sheep Station – in Australia the farm or property where they raise sheep is called a Sheep Station.

Sheila – a girl, a woman

Shilling – also known as a dina (pronounced deenah) – pre decimal currency equivalent to ten cents

Shot through – cleared off, run away, took off

Shot through like a Bondi Tram - When the trams were running to Bondi, they were known for travelling fast. Someone who runs fast. Just imagine being late for the tram taking you somewhere and seeing it dwindling in size as it sped away into the distance.

Shoulda – should have

Sickie – a day off work when you pretend to be ill.

Sixpence – in the old currency and now 5c, five cents.

Six o'clock swill – in Australia at this time in the 1950's the hotels closed at 6 o'clock so all the drinkers would order a few beers each and do their best to drink them all before they were turfed out of the pub.

Skeeter – someone who is small like a mosquito, shortened to skeeter. Can also be called flea, a little insect.

Smart Aleck – someone who knows everything but knows nothing, a know all.

Smiths Chips – a popular brand of salted chips made by the Smiths Company

Snags – sausages, Bruce and Greta's favourite food

Snitched – stole something. Or to tell someone about you.

Sod – an old sod, and old bloke or man

Sozzled – drunk, inebriated

SP Bookie – Starting Price betting - an off course bookmaker who takes the bets of the punters on the horses, trots and the dogs. Then illegal gambling.

Steinlager – a New Zealand make of beer, very cold, very strong, which may account for the way Kiwis act. Not as good as Tooheys though.

Stone the bloody crows – an Australian exclamation, one is exasperated.

Stout – a dark heavily malted beer

Strike a light – get moving

Strine – the Australian way of pronouncing words

Sun - the Daily newspaper called the Sun.

Suitcase — a valise or port

Swell — a person filled with self-importance

Sydney Morning Herald — a Sydney newspaper

T

Tank — an Australian country term for an earthen dam to catch runoff or rain water.

Tasman Sea — part of the Pacific Ocean named by the explorer Abel Tasman. It washes the shores of Bondi Beach and also across the way, just over the horizon to New Zealand.

The Gap — the entrance to Sydney Harbour, through two towering cliffs

The Man from Snowy River — the best poem in the world written by Banjo Patterson.

The Sallies — The Salvation Army

Thit — New Zealand for, that

Toff - Australian term for an upper class person, not a worker.

Tooheys, Tooheys KB, a maker of beer. Tastes real good.

Too right — when someone agrees with you, absolutely etc

Tooth merchant — someone who likes their food

Town — meaning the city. The Big Smoke, Sydney.

Trots — the horse races where the horses trot and not gallop. The horse's rider sits in a two wheeled buggy. The horse trots as fast as he can to get away from the buggy but it stays there firmly behind him.

Tucker — Australian, food

Turfed out — thrown out

U

Ute – utility truck, a two doored car with a truck's tray on the back

V

Vegemite – a savoury vitamin enriched spread for bread, toast etc. Note; it does not have sugar in it. It is not sweet.

W

Wadderyah know – what do you – in other words 'what do you know?'.... surprise.

Wags – Larrikins, funny fellows, jokesters

Wafers - a form of ice cream served between two wafers made from cornflower, like a thick ice cream sandwich.

Wagging – playing truant

Walkabout – the aboriginal people have a tradition of being nomads and they sometimes leave a place and go visit somewhere else. Bruce reckons most probably a form of claustrophobia

Wee – Scottish for small, little

Wee Wully – small Willy, little Willy, little William, young Willy.

Whet your whistle – moisten your lips, with a drink of beer of course.

Whisky chasers – seasoned drinkers sometimes drink a beer then also swallow a glass or a shot of whisky.

Wingers – a position that lighter and faster men play in Rugby Union football. One is on each side of the field and they are usually the fastest men on the team

Wonky – ill fitted and off balance

Woodah – would have

Wot – Australian for, what

Wouldja — Australian for, would you.

Wullie — Scots for Willy, an affectionate shortening of the name William to Willy, pronounced Wullie.

Wuz - was

Y

Ya — you

Yah — you

Yeh — yes

Yer - you

Yis — New Zealand for, yes

Yiz - you

Yobboe, yobboes — man, men

Youse — you, most probably more than one a group of people.

The Author and illustrator

Experts in writing teach that it is simpler to avoid using accents and colloquial speech however in these stories I have ignored that. The speech of many Australians in the 1950's especially in the country regions was different and I have attempted to show how some of the people spoke way back then. I hope you can get the gist of what the characters in this book are talking about although I suspect that readers from overseas will be flummoxed. I am recording history you see!

The first book has enjoyed some critical acclaim and the comments seem to be that the readers could not put the book down and rushed through it and enjoyed it. Each book takes months to write and illustrate. It therefore somewhat of a shock to hear that many readers scramble through its pages in about four hours! Oh, well I will just have to write more then.

If you would like to read more of my books then go to Amazon and search for Steve McGregor or Adventures of a Jackeroo. All the books published are there as eBooks and the book price is very reasonable.

A comment on the illustrations. I have studied Commercial Art at East Sydney technical College in the early 1960's and also tried my hand later at oil painting and watercolours. My style is a simple, yet an expressive one, characterised by bright washes of water colour and black ink outlines. Basically, I try to keep it simple and avoid fiddling. The effect is what I am after. As long as I get close to what I what then I will stop at that.

The illustrations are usually completed before the chapter is written. They are sometimes roughed out in pencil and then inked in with a waterproof ink. Coloured inks are used for the figures and the backgrounds usually completed in water colour washes.

I do hope you enjoy reading the books and let me know what you think. Stevemcgregor3@bigpond.com also www.stephenmcgregorartist.com.au

**Steve McGregor,
St. Ives, NSW, Australia**

Other books
written and illustrated
by Steve McGregor

Suitable for children 6 years of age onwards

A young Aboriginal boy called Wally living in the country area of Australia. Ideal for children and also young adults living in Australia or overseas. These delightful books are an introduction to how the original people of Australia may have lived only a short time ago. There are five books in the series.

Wally and the Boomerang.

Wally the Warrior:

Wally and the Hunt for the Giant Bunyip

Wally Goes Fishing

Wally and the Poachers

Teenagers

Eddie Mulligan is a mischievous lad of about eight years and he and his mate Piggy Andrews share in many adventures and escapades. Set in the 1950's in Australia these charming books will delight children.

Adventures of Eddie Mulligan – It's hard being Eddie Mulligan – Book 1

Adventures of Eddie Mulligan – Eddie makes his first mistake – Book 2

Adults

The two books are about Bruce a hapless and gormless youth. Not enjoying school he started work as a trainee property manager (a Jackeroo) on a sheep station way out west. The second book tells of the adventures of Bruce who tiring of the life in the bush decides to start work at the Auckland Hotel near to his favourite place, Bondi Beach. See both of these books on Amazon as an eBook

Adventures of a Jackeroo – Book 1

Adventures of Bruce from Bondi – Book 2

Contact Steve by email
if you need any information on the books
stevemcgregor3@bigpond.com

Or see the web site
www.stephenmcgregorartist.com.au